THE GIRLS OF CANBY HALL

HAPPY BIRTHDAY, JANE

EMILY CHASE

D0595909

SCHOLASTIC INC.
New York Toronto London Auckland Sydney

ISBN 0-590-41516-6

12 11 10 9 8 7 6 5 4 3 2 1   8 9/8 0 1 2 3/9

Printed in the U.S.A.   01

First Scholastic printing, June 1988

HAPPY BIRTHDAY, JANE

THE GIRLS OF CANBY HALL

Roommates
Our Roommate Is Missing
You're No Friend of Mine
Keeping Secrets
Summer Blues
Best Friends Forever
Four Is a Crowd
The Big Crush
Boy Trouble
Make Me a Star
With Friends Like That
Who's the New Girl?
Here Come the Boys
What's a Girl To Do?
To Tell the Truth
Three of a Kind
Graduation Day
Making Friends
One Boy Too Many
Something Old, Something New
Friends Times Three
Party Time!
Troublemaker
The Almost Summer Carnival
But She's So Cute
Princess Who?
The Ghost of Canby Hall
Help Wanted!
The Roommate and the Cowboy
Happy Birthday, Jane

CHAPTER ONE

Jane Barrett sat up in bed startled, awakened by the chirping of the phone. In her dream it had been a blue jay on the window sill of her room, 407 Baker, at Canby Hall, a girls' boarding school in Massachusetts. The chirping persisted as she groped among the piles of clothes surrounding her bed. She followed the sound to a bleating blue shetland sweater and found the receiver.

"Hello, this is Jane. Oh, hi, Mother."

Jane climbed back under her antique cross-stitched quilt. "No, it's sunny here. More Indian Summer, I guess." She looked toward the ceiling. "Cloudy in Boston? Oh." Had her mother roused her from the luxury of a Saturday morning sleep-in to give her the weather report? Jane brushed her long blonde hair from her face and began twisting one of the strands, her head nodding, a blank, sleepy expression on her face.

1

As her mother chatted on, Jane broke slowly into a smile, then a wide grin. "That's right, just a week away. Just think. Sixteen! I'll be sixteen."

The smile clouded over as Jane's mother began elaborating birthday plans. Why didn't Jane bring her roommates — and her friend Cary Slade — to Boston for the weekend? And any others she wanted to include. They could reserve that long table in the sunroom of the country club and have a lovely dinner party on Saturday night.

Jane winced, thinking how Cary, who was lead guitarist in Oakley Prep's rock band, Ambulance, would feel about the boring sounds of the club's orchestra, with its tuxedoed violinist and *accordion* player. Strictly from Muzak.

The last time she'd taken her friends to Boston — for the anniversary of the landing of the Barrett ancestors in America — the situation had been pretty tense and awkward for a while. However, thanks to her roommates, things had loosened up.

Although that party was a success, the Barretts' elegant country club was *so* stuffy that Jane certainly did not want to spend this most important birthday there.

"Er, Mother, if you don't mind, I think we'd have more fun celebrating here. I mean I appreciate . . ."

Jane could hear the disappointment in her

mother's voice. She hated to let her family down. They were all very close; her father, David French Barrett, a highly respected banker, her mother, who was a noted patron of the arts, and her older sister Charlotte, who was at Smith.

Jane felt guilty when her mother, with a resigned sigh, told her she'd just send a check — a check so that Jane could give her own party. After all, it was *her* day and certainly she understood. Would three hundred dollars be enough?

"Three hundred dollars? Mother, that, would be great!"

"Good. We'd spend more here," came the crisp answer. "And this way you can plan the day exactly the way you want it."

"Oh, mother!" Jane was breathless. "That's wonderful. You and Father are always so generous." Then her mother suggested that she and Jane's father could visit her on Sunday the day after, for a post-birthday dinner at the Greenleaf Inn.

"If you're sure you won't be coming home," came Gloria Barrett's voice through the receiver, "I'll send the check Express Mail, along with your gift. Call me when you receive it."

"Oh, please. Nothing more," Jane protested. "The check alone is too much."

"This is something I want you to have," said her mother. "It's appropriate for this special birthday. Be sure to call me when it arrives."

Mrs. Barrett sounded excited about the gift. A little worried, too. But then she always fussed over any present she gave, saying things like, "Take it back if you don't like it," which Jane knew she didn't mean.

After Jane put down the phone, she ruffled through her overstuffed desk drawer, found a yellow legal pad and pencil under some Polaroids of her with her sister Charlotte at her school, an empty radio battery package and two Twix Bar wrappers. She plumped the pillows behind her and got ready to jot down ideas for the birthday. But instead she sat there with the blank paper, the pencil eraser between her teeth. Three hundred dollars! That would take a lot of thinking. Sometimes life was easier without so many choices.

Jane stared out the window at the cloudless blue sky, the trees in front of Baker tinged with the first colors of September. She was glad to have the room quiet; her roommates had left early. Toby was, no doubt, horseback riding with Randy Crowell, who had a ranch down the road. Andy was probably doing ballet stretch exercises or aerobic dancing at the gym. Sometimes her lively roommates made her feel lazy.

At times — like right now — Jane felt a little pampered. Andy had grown up working in her parents' restaurant. Before leaving for

Canby Hall, Toby had helped her widowed father on his cattle ranch. What had Jane ever done to earn all that had been lavished on her: the lovely clothes from the best stores; the private lessons in piano, dancing, fencing, and tennis; going to plays, concerts, guided tours through every museum on the East Coast. She'd taken this enviable life much for granted until becoming close to Toby and Andy. She wondered how they'd feel if they had three hundred dollars to spend on a birthday, trying to picture how they'd spend it. Planning this special day wasn't going to be easy. She might have to have some help.

"A birthday? Terrific!" Andy took off her aerobic shoes and stretched out on her bedspread. Its diagonal earth-toned stripes clashed with the pink flowered jeans she wore over her maroon leotard. "Nothing like a party to get the school year rolling." Hands behind her dark curly head, she raised her legs straight up toward the ceiling and stared at her feet, curling her toes in the feet of the tights. "How come I didn't remember you were born in September?"

Jane laughed. "If you remember, last year at this point the three of us were hardly speaking." She shook her blonde head. "Can you believe all the fuss I made about wanting to live alone? Think of all the crazy times I would have missed."

"Think of all the closet space you'd have," teased Andy. She reached down by the side of her bed and tossed her roommate's paisley Liberty scarf back to Jane's corner of the room. It landed on the blue and gray Persian rug beside her bed.

"I know what a selfish snob you thought I was."

"Ms. Boston Cream Pie," Andy snickered. "Rich and messy."

"Oh, you!" Jane giggled, and got out of bed.

"But honestly, Andy, sometimes around you and Toby I still feel, uh — well, a little spoiled."

"Hey, don't be loony. You are the soul of generosity." Andy grinned. "I'll vouch for that. Provided, that is, I'm invited to your birthday."

"You're not only invited, you're on the planning committee," said Jane. Taking Andy's teasing hint, she picked up the scarf and folded it, then sat on the bed and began matching and rolling socks. "Can you imagine, my mother is sending me three hundred dollars for all of us to spend!"

"You're joking. Three Benjamin Franklins?"

"Mother says that's less than she would have spent at home. She wanted to give a dinner party in Boston — at the country club."

"Wow, I'm glad you talked her out of that.

City girls like me don't belong in *country* clubs."

"Come on, Andy. You're the kind of person who fits perfectly everyplace. Like a . . . like a leotard."

"And sometimes gets just as sweaty."

Jane smiled to acknowledge the joke. "What would everyone like to do? The three of us. And Cary, of course. You might want to invite Matt. And Toby could ask Randy. Or Neal." Jane's former boy friend Neal — short for Cornelius Worthington III — had celebrated birthdays with her since they were children. It would be strange this year, seeing him with Toby, of whom he seemed quite fond. An unlikely match, but a good one.

"We're all so different," Jane went on. "Figuring out something that's fun for everyone might be a problem."

Andy sat up straight on the edge of her bed. Her dark eyes glowed. "No problem at all. New York City Ballet is performing *Giselle* at Lincoln Center next weekend."

"Ouch!" giggled Jane. "Can you see Cary squirming through that?"

"Not squirming. Sleeping," Andy admitted.

"I was thinking of going to some beautiful restaurant. Then taking in a play or concert."

"I've spent my life working in a restaurant. You think it's a treat to *eat* in one?"

"This isn't going to be easy."

"But if a person *has* to have a problem,"

Andy remarked, "having three hundred dollars to spend on a birthday seems like a pretty good one to me."

Jane shrugged. "As I said before. Sometimes you make me feel spoiled."

Andy hopped up from the bed and began dancing a little hard rock number, bellowing as she pranced. "Rotten spoiled, baby, rotten *spy*-iled." She made up the words as she went along, ending the song like an MTV star, arms out, legs splayed. "If you feel spoiled, baby, it's cuz I'm too *fresh*."

Jane doubled up laughing and pelted the performer with a ball of rolled up socks.

"Whew, shades of summer," Toby said as she burst through the door, tennis racket in hand. She was wearing white shorts and a green T-shirt, damp in spots between her shoulders. Her red hair, held by a matching sweatband, curled into wet ringlets. She laid the racket on her rainbow bedspread, then leaned down to take off her new K-Swiss tennis shoes, bought at an end-of-summer sale in Greenleaf.

"Have a good game?" asked Jane.

"Just a workout," said Toby. "Randy's getting me in shape for the team tryouts. He's pretty sure I'll make it this time. At least as an alternate."

"Hey, great," said Andy.

Toby stood up and stretched, then flexed into a deep knee bend. "If these joints of mine hold together. Right now I feel like I'm a hundred years old."

"Randy's a tough teacher, eh?"

"He doesn't mean to be," Toby sighed. "It's just that he hits so hard and fast. I kill myself to get to the ball."

She collapsed onto the floor, resting her back against the bed. "I'm afraid if I don't keep the rally going, he'll get bored."

"Randy bored with tennis?" said Andy. "That's like Baryshnikov being bored with ballet."

"Olivier with the theater," said Jane.

"Anyway, it's great working out with Randy. He really picks up my timing."

Andy reached over to her desk. "By the way, Jane," she said, "since it's almost your birthday — and since you missed breakfast — I have a present for you." She handed Jane a small square wrapped in a yellow paper napkin. "Blueberry surprise."

"Ummm. That's very thoughtful of you Andy. I *am* hungry, come to think of it."

"They're real blueberries. That's the surprise," quipped Andy. "The cafeteria manager must be out sick. The scrambled eggs didn't ooze today."

"And the bacon didn't oink," Toby added. She slid her racket into its case and put it under the bed. "But what's this about your birthday? Why didn't you tell us?"

"It's not until next Saturday," said Jane.

There's still time to buy out the stores in Greenleaf, should you care to. I have my list of suggestions right here." She rolled the crumbs of the cake-square in the napkin and put it on her desk, then held up the yellow pad, which still had no writing on it.

"That's not much help," said Toby.

"Seriously, I don't want anything for my birthday — except for the most wonderful party in the world. Which the three of us have got to plan. Right now!" She took the pencil and began to write.

CHAPTER TWO

Well come on, you two. Speak up. I'm wide open for ideas. You know I can't plan this party all by myself." Almost a half hour had gone by, and Jane's yellow pad was still blank, except for the words "Birthday Ideas" under which she had doodled a three-layer birthday cake. It had roses on the sides and candles around the second layer. Toby and Andy had contributed nothing more than "Uh, let's see . . ." and a couple of "How abouts . . ." with no ideas filling in the blank spaces.

"This is hard," said Toby. "I mean, I don't want to be responsible. What if we choose something you don't like to do?"

"And ruin your big, most important birthday," said Andy.

"No chance," said Jane. "This day is going to be perfection, no matter what we decide. She smiled, her eyes taking on a dreamy expression. "Just think, sixteen. And New York's so beautiful this time of year."

Toby and Andy looked at each other. "New York? Where in New York?"

"New York, New York," said Jane.

"How about a baseball game at Shea Stadium?" suggested Andy. "The Chicago Cubs might be playing. Top the day off with a few rides at Coney Island.

"Please," said Jane, with an almost visible shudder. "*Not* Coney Island."

"Maybe The Bronx Zoo?" said Toby, who loved animals. "That's a place I've always wanted to see. Especially the snake house."

Jane looked horrified, but didn't comment on Toby's suggestion. "I mean the *City*," said Jane.

"You mean," said Andy, "that you're wide open to ideas. Choose any old place, as long as it's mid-town Manhattan."

"I didn't say that," said Jane. "But there's so much to do. We could spend the morning at the Whitney Museum. Go to the matinee at the Metropolitan Opera."

"You must be very sure of Cary's love," said Andy. "Sounds like you want to test his breaking point in the culture marathon."

Jane sighed. "I guess you're right. I'm so used to Neal. He used to love afternoons in New York. After the opera matinee, we'd always go to the record store and buy a tape of the arias."

"That's a nice idea," Toby said. She made a mental note to go to the library and check out a few books on the opera, maybe a few tapes. She would read them and play them in secret. Her roommates might tease her if they saw her boning up on things Neal was interested in. But sometimes — without meaning to — he made her feel so *uncivilized* — at least if you thought of civilization in Boston, rather than, say, Texas, terms.

Andy, who was sitting cross-legged on the floor, got up to stretch. "Couldn't we have a big city day in Boston? It's a lot closer."

"But then," Jane objected, "Mother would insist we stay for dinner. And then we're right back where we started — hobnobbing at the country club."

"I think what we need," sighed Andy, "is a little inspiration. Maybe a Coke or a root beer. I have some change for the machine — for a change."

"Anybody for lunch?" asked Toby. "I'm starving."

"We just finished breakfast," said Jane.

"*You* just finished breakfast," said Andy. "I'm with you, Toby. How about a juicy hamburger at the diner?"

"Well, in that case, you talked me into it," said Jane.

"You're always hungry," Andy teased, "for the sight of Cary Slade."

Jane blushed slightly and brushed back her

bangs. "I can't deny that," she said, bounding off the bed. She picked up yesterday's designer jeans from her pile of just-folded clothes — light gray Calvin Kleins — then tucked in a long-sleeved pink and gray striped shirt from another pile. "Voilà!" she said. "Instant dressing."

"Saves a lot of time when you don't have to go to the closet," Toby observed.

"We need Cary's ideas, anyway," said Jane, ignoring Toby's crack. "You know, the male point of view."

She pulled up the quilted spread to make the bed; all the rolled socks and stacks of folded clothes fell to the floor. "Oh, well," she laughed. "Serves me right for trying. I'll know better next time!"

Toby grabbed her cowgirl hat, Andy her over-the-shoulder envelope purse. Both roommates shrugged as they stepped over the clothes on the way out the door.

Toby and Andy slipped into the front side of the high-backed diner booth, leaving Jane the side where she could see the whole restaurant — and let her eyes follow Cary as he waited on each table. The Greaf (Greenleaf with a few letters missing from the sign) was quieter than usual because the Chamber of Commerce had just finished a pancake breakfast in the theater parking lot. The girls could see out the window — business people and their spouses folding up tables and chairs as the last customers finished up paper plates full of "all you can eat" hotcakes.

Jane stared at Cary until he looked up from his order pad. She watched his face break into a wide grin. "Be right with you."

"Hi, Cary," said Toby and Andy in unison as Cary approached the table.

"All three of you," said Cary. "To what do I owe this honor?"

"You know," said Jane, "it's the triple treat. Like a three-decker ice cream cone. And we need your thoughts," said Jane.

"Thoughts?" he said, placing three glasses of water on the table. "Well, you're in luck. It just so happens they're on special today. Comes with soup or salad at a dollar off."

"Sounds good," said Andy. "I'll have mine well done."

"Sorry," said Cary, "Only my burgers are well done. My thoughts are rare."

"We'll have three burgers then," said Jane. She grinned ear to ear. "Say, you're in a great mood today."

"Matter of fact I am," said Cary. "Guess who's playing for the Hillsboro Homecoming?"

"Ambulance!" said Jane. "That's terrific!"

"The Print Outs had to cancel. Guitarist has mono."

"Too bad," said Jane. "But that's a nice break for you."

"One of these days," said Andy, "you'll be booked all over the state."

"Let's hope so," said Cary and tore off their ticket.

"Well done for everyone?" he asked.

"Medium for me," said Toby.

"And three root beers, right?" It seemed Cary had barely left the table when he returned with three steaming burgers. With a flourish he set a place before each girl. "So what's up?" he said. "Besides catsup?" He somersaulted a bottle of Heinz and placed it on the table.

"We need your advice on my birthday," said Jane, taking the pickle off the bun.

"That's right, it's coming right up!" said Cary. His face darkened a little. "I suppose you'll spend the weekend in Boston."

"No, we've decided to celebrate here," said Jane. "Mother is sending me a check for three hundred dollars, to spend for any kind of a party we want. The three of us have been racking our brains — "

"Three hundred dollars? Hey, terrific. That should be no problem. The Space Cadets are appearing next week at Musicland. I guess that ought to wrap up your birthday plans."

"The Space Cadets?"

"I'll admit they're pretty far out. You earth dwellers may not yet be aware of their arrival on the planet. So much the better, think what you can look forward to!"

"Cary, uh, you know I love rock concerts — especially yours — but on my birthday I sort of pictured . . ." Jane couldn't finish the sentence; she could see the disappointment on Cary's face. So few people realized how deeply he felt about his music. Jane felt she understood, but she couldn't always share his enthusiasm, which sometimes bordered on the fanatic.

"I'll get your check," he said quietly. "Anybody need anything else?"

As Cary left the table another tall figure moved up to the edge of the booth. Andy looked up. "Matt!" She smoothed her hair. "Come join us."

"Just had breakfast," he said, "One hundred and fifteen pancakes. But I'll join you for a lemonade."

"You're just in time,'" said Jane. "I want you to come to my birthday celebration next Saturday."

"It just so happens," said Matt, pretending to check an invisible date book, "that I am free that day. Or night. Which is it?"

"That's the trouble," said Andy. "We don't know. Either. Maybe both. We can't decide what to do."

"Got any suggestions?" said Toby. "We have far too many possibilities. With three hundred dollars to spend, thanks to Jane's mother."

Matt's dark eyes got a faraway look. 'Three

hundred dollars? I sure know what *I'd* do. Something I've been wanting for a long, long time. But, up to now," he said, catching Jane's eye, "I've never had the cash."

The group focused on Matt as he spoke softly and slowly, drawing in his mind the ideal day. "I'd pack a fancy picnic lunch. Take a tape player with my favorite tapes. My swim trunks and a towel. A fishing rod. And a case of Creme soda . . ."

"And?" said Andy.

"I'd rent a big sailboat, the kind with a cabin, and down the river I'd go."

"Sailing!" said Toby. "That *would* be fun." She'd never been on a boat of any kind.

"The sailing part would be fine," said Matt, "except I don't know how. But it's the tying-up part I like. Bobbing up and down so peaceful, with no one around but the trout."

"I'd prefer my trout with almonds under glass," said Jane. "Like at Chez Monique. Mmmm, anyone for a five-course, four-star dinner?" But since the group was full of hamburgers and pancakes, no one spoke up.

"Well, fine, let's do that, then. Chez Monique."

"A restaurant in any language is still a restaurant," said Andy. "And I for one am sick of them."

"Fancy dinners are sort of boring," said Toby, trying to head off another evening that threatened finger bowls.

"Thumbs down," said Matt. "I'd have to wear a tie."

At this point Cary returned, white cloth in hand, to wipe down the table. "We're thinking about Chez Monique for my birthday," Jane told him.

"*We're* thinking?" said Andy. You mean *you're* thinking. We've all nixed that pup."

"Hey, wait a minute," said Jane with ice cubes in her voice, "whose birthday is this, anyway? On my day we should do what *I* want."

"You're right," said Cary, taking off his paper waiter's hat and bowing. "Even if we gag on it."

"Now that's what I call democracy!" said Andy.

"Boooo!" said Matt.

"Boring!" said Toby.

Jane bit her lip. The teasing had gone a little far. "Okay, okay, I give up. Cancel Chez Monique." She knew her friends well enough to know that if she insisted on having her way, they'd all put on smiling faces and pretend to be having a fantastic evening. And that pretending would ruin everything. That's what was so terrific about each one of these special people, their honest way of dealing with each other. Like booing!

She forced a smile, "As I said, I'm open to any *democratic* suggestions."

"Having now returned to democracy," said

Andy, "why don't we put the birthday to a vote?"

"Sure. Why not?" said Toby. "How about a secret ballot? And since none of us seems to agree, why not draw the winner from a hat? *This* hat." She took off her cowgirl hat and put it in the center of the table.

The restaurant was empty now except for the back booth. Cary went to the cash register and brought back a pad of paper, handing each voter a slip. They passed his order-taking pencil amongst themselves, each, except Matt, pausing a moment before writing the birthday choice.

Cary went first, writing "Chez Jardin."

Jane, covering the slip with her left hand wrote "Rock concert."

Andy wrote "Ballet," then crossed it out for "Baseball game."

Toby wrote "Barbecue in the park by the zoo."

When the slips were in the hat, Toby handed it to Jane. "Never let it be said that you didn't get to choose your birthday!"

Jane laughed and reached for one of the folded slips, then stopped. "Wait, we forgot about Neal. You'd like to invite him, wouldn't you, Toby?"

Toby colored a little. "Sure, if that's okay."

"Then you should fill out his slip."

Toby thought for a few seconds, then wrote

"Baseball game." Neal had mentioned his passion for the Sox on their last date.

Jane closed her eyes, "May the best wish win!" and slowly drew out the slip.

It was Matt's, marked "Sailing."

CHAPTER THREE

I t's going to be great fun!" said Toby, putting sunscreen on her pale, freckled legs. "I can hardly wait till tomorrow."

The girls of 407, in shorts, were stretched out on the lawn in front of Baker, using their Friday afternoon to enjoy the warm September sun. "This might be one of the last warm weekends," said Jane. "Let's hope our Indian summer hot spell holds."

" 'It's always fair weather when good friends get together,' " said Andy, who was putting clear polish on her fingernails and toenails, the polish bottle balanced on her knees.

"Who said that — Shakespeare?" asked Toby. The other two ignored her, knowing it certainly wasn't Shakespeare, but not having a clue about who it was — if anybody.

"Neal called this morning," Toby said. "He has a great boat lined up. We're lucky his friend rents out his yacht on weekends. It's got a cabin with bunks and a kitchen and everything. Uh, I mean a galley."

"Thank goodness Neal knows how to sail," said Jane.

"Well, of course, we could just stay tied up in the anchorage all day," said Andy. "That's Matt's idea of sailing, anyway."

"I think we all ought to learn a little bit about boating," said Toby. "We can't let Neal do all the work."

"He can be captain," said Andy, "and give us orders."

"Not to people who don't know a martingale from a mizzenmast."

"Hey," said Andy, "you didn't learn that on any Texas ranch."

"On a ranch a martingale is something you train horses with. On a boat, it's a spar on the bowsprit."

"Say, we're impressed!" said Jane.

Toby felt her warm cheeks. Was it the sun or was she blushing a little? "I went to the library after lunch," she admitted. "Checked out Royce's *Sailing Illustrated*. Which I'll be glad to lend you." She brushed back her red curls. "What a goldmine of information. You could spend a week just learning about knots."

"Oh, I know about knots," said Jane. "That's how fast the boat goes."

"Unless someone throws you a rope," said Toby. "If you fasten the boat the wrong way, you could all of a sudden be at sea."

"Breezing along at fifteen knots, right?" said Andy. She took several bottles of nail polish from her straw bag and began painting her toenails in different colors. The big toe pink, the second blue-green, the third a pale yellow.

"What in the world?" asked Jane, laughing.

"Rainbow toes," said Andy. "Aren't they beautiful?"

"Well . . . ," said Jane.

"If I'm going to be a professional ballet dancer, my feet will be my fortune. I might as well get them used to the glamorous life." She put purple on the fourth and pink on the baby toe.

"Nice," said Toby, with genuine admiration.

"Want to try some?" asked Andy. "I'm going to do the same with my fingers."

"Thanks," said Toby, "but I don't think rainbows are quite my style. Except for my bedspread, of course." Toby had put the rainbow bedspread on her bed again this year, along with the mysterious tea bag, which she hung on the ceiling above her pillow. Was it the same tea bag as last year? Or was it a tea bag at all? Maybe it was a packet of magic herbs, for all Jane and Andy knew. Because Toby wasn't telling.

"This is going to be one all-time great birthday," said Andy. "Sailing really *is* the best choice for all of us." She started in on her fingernails. "I mean, we can sort of combine everyone's wishes. Take some tapes of everyone's favorite music — from Bach to Rock. And we can bring along Jane's five-course meal."

"Maybe a portable barbecue, too," said Toby.

"We can play baseball on the beach," said Jane.

"Take a walk in the woods and see the birds and animals," said Toby.

"But no snakes!" said Jane.

"Okay, no snakes," Toby promised.

Jane adjusted the straps of her tank top to make sure her shoulders browned evenly. "It's lucky Neal's coming tonight with his car. We have a lot of shopping to do. Let's see, for lunch some croissants and brie and pate . . ."

"Speak English, will you?" said Toby. "I'd like to know what I'm eating."

"That's sort of like smelly cheese and liverwurst," said Andy, "on a squishy roll."

Toby felt like saying "Yuk," but remembering these weird foods were for Jane's birthday, said instead, "Sounds good!"

"How about some hot dogs and potato chips?" said Andy, seeing Toby's look of disappointment.

"Why not?" said Jane. "Say, I have an idea. Why not have a food festival? Everyone can bring their favorite foods."

"We can eat all day long," said Toby with a grin.

"But what you eat, you cook," cautioned Jane.

"Umm, steak and baked potatoes," said Toby. "With corn on the cob."

"Salad," said Andy. "Heaps of green salad. With tomatoes and blue cheese dressing. The kind my father serves."

"Matt can catch me a trout," said Jane. "We'll cook it with almond butter."

"We?" teased Andy, remembering some of Jane's earlier attempts at cooking. "And how are we going to catch trout in the ocean?"

"Are we sailing in the ocean?" asked Jane. "I sort of pictured a sheltered bay. Or a peaceful river cruise."

"The boat is anchored in a small bay near Gloucester," said Toby. "Neal says there's a river near there. So we can have our choice, I guess."

"Maybe we can take a vote," said Andy.

"Oh, no, not democracy again!" said Jane.

Toby laughed, and sprang to her feet. "No reason why we can't do all three."

"Sure," said Andy. "This is a birthday-o-rama."

Brushing off her shorts, Toby felt the bumpy lines the grass had made on her legs.

"Meantime I've got to get back to studying."

"On Friday afternoon?" Andy said. "Come on, now!"

"I mean the book on sailing," said Toby. "Neal will be here around seven. So I've only got a few hours to get shipshape. Or ship smart. Whatever you call it." She padded away barefoot, leaving Jane and Andy looking at each other. Jane raised a questioning eyebrow; Andy answered her glance with a shrug.

Toby popped up from the bed and put a marker in the *Sailing Illustrated*. Five-thirty already. Better hurry. She smoothed her rainbow bedspread and as she plumped her pillows, she raised her eyes to the tea bag that hung from the ceiling, as if asking for luck. She grabbed her towel, which was folded over the end of the bed, took a shampoo bottle from the dresser drawer, and headed down the hall.

In the shower, as the warm water rained over her shoulders, she felt a glow of excitement. In two hours or less Neal would be there — for the entire weekend. There would be hours on end for them to be together, the way she imagined every day she was away from him. First the big birthday celebration on that fantastic yacht. Or did he say yawl? Or maybe it was "Yawl will love the yacht." At any rate, Neal had sounded enthusiastic.

They would play tennis on Sunday. Perhaps

go for a ride at Randy Crowell's ranch. But
tonight, of course, they had to shop for the
party. First things first.

As the water streamed over her head, Toby
cupped her hand and poured shampoo into it.
It was the kind Jane used, that smelled like
fresh coconut. Jane had brought several bottles from Boston and had given one to each of
her roommates. Her mother bought it by the
case from her exclusive hair salon. Toby asked
herself if she should blow her hair dry with
a roller brush like Jane did, maybe try something a little fancier, instead of letting her
natural curls have their own way. She wondered, as she had so many other times, how
Neal, who was used to the style of society girls
like Jane — could be interested in a plain-
spoken, down-to-earth girl from a Texas
ranch.

As she turned off the shower, a chilling
thought came to mind. She hadn't studied
that sailing book nearly enough.

For days Toby had pictured Neal's surprised smile as he watched her rigging the
mainsail, ballooning the jib to catch the down-
wind, swinging the tiller wide when he called
"Come about!" Now she could see his disappointment as she floundered around the
deck like a fresh-caught fish.

She stepped out and dried her tender skin,
which was slightly pink — and a bit more

freckled — from the afternoon sun. Wrapping the towel around her wet curls, she slipped into the old shirt she wore as a robe in warm weather.

And that was another thing, she worried. What if the weather took a turn for the worse, and Neal was caught in a storm with five novice sailors, single-handedly trying to maneuver his friend's expensive boat? Toby saw sails flapping wildly, the boat listing, water pouring over the side. She shuddered as she returned to 407.

When she had settled back on her bed, a glance out the window reassured her. There was no sign of what in Texas they called a "mackerel sky," a bumpy blanket of high clouds that heralds a change in the weather. In fact, there wasn't a single cloud. The autumn sky was a brilliant blue.

Toby opened the sailing book, hoping to catch a few more terms before dinner. She began muttering the words as she memorized them: "Halyard, batten, gooseneck."

Andy bounced in, pounced on her bed, and watched two of her stuffed animals fall to the floor. "What's with you?"

"Cringle, bunt, reef," Toby said.

"Hey, Jane, come quick," Andy said. "Maybe it's something she ate. . . ."

As Jane entered the room, Toby continued solemnly, "Lanyard, leach, jibe."

Jane gave a groan and tossed her sunning towel at her roommate. "Toby, speak to us. I mean, speak to us like a Texan."

By this time Toby was thoroughly enjoying herself. She ran her finger down the glossary and said, "Luff me on the lee to the lubber-line!"

"Say," said Andy, "that's not a bad song title," "Luff me or lee me, baby!, dah de dah dee dah."

"Maybe Cary could use it," Jane chimed in.

"What do you know, Jane?" Andy nodded toward Toby's book. "Our friend Toby's getting nautical again. Going to take the words right out of our mouths."

"Or the wind right out of our sails," said Jane.

"Seriously," said Toby, although she was laughing, "We should try to learn a little about sailing before Neal comes. He can't take us out to sea calling, "Unhitch the thing-amabob and toss me the whatsis."

"Can't we just use plain English like *rope* and *sail* and *deck*?"

"Which deck?" said Toby. "Fore, main, aft, or poop?"

"Poop?" asked Jane, incredulous.

"And which rope, the outhaul or the down-haul?"

"I give up," said Andy. "I can see you're

way ahead of us." She took the book, which
Toby had laid on her bed. She opened it at
random, studied the page, then burst out
laughing, "Why Jane, I'll bet you don't even
know how to 'scandalize a gaff.' "

"Scandalize?" asked Jane, with a mock
shocked look on her face.

"Sounds like something no one would do in
Boston," Toby chuckled.

"In Boston no one ever makes a gaff," said
Andy.

"That's enough about Boston," said Jane,
but she was smiling.

" 'Scandalizing a gaff,' " said Andy, reading
from the pages, "is an emergency measure.
You 'set up the topping lift and release the
peak halyard.' That 'reduces the sail area.'
Understand?"

"See what I mean?" said Toby. "I sure hope
we don't run into any emergency. We'd probably sink before Neal could translate for us."

"Well, let's not worry," said Jane. "It looks
like tomorrow will be a perfect day. I'm more
concerned at this point about getting all the
birthday supplies. Do you have your lists
ready?"

"Lists?" asked Toby.

"Remember, this morning I said we all could
bring our favorite foods. This is the oppor-
tunity of a lifetime. You'd better be prepared
for tonight's raid on the Greenleaf A&P." She

rummaged in her desk for the yellow pad.

"Wow," said Andy. "We'd better get busy. I think my appetite just woke up."

The phone rang and all three girls moved toward it with hopeful looks on their faces. Jane, being closest, answered. "Oh, yes, Merry. Thank you. Sure, I'll be right over."

Jane put down the receiver, "Meredith says a package for me was express-delivered to her apartment. That must be the birthday surprise my mother is sending. *And* the check." She gave her bangs a couple of quick strokes with a brush from the dresser. "I'm anxious to see my gift. It was so sweet of Mother to send something extra, along with the party money. Now I feel guilty about not going home for my birthday."

"I'm sure your mother understands," said Andy, although she didn't seem too sure of her words. Jane's mother had never struck Andy as the understanding type. "Any idea what you're getting?"

"Not a one," said Jane. "But the gift sounds rather special. When Mother told me about it, she sounded a little worried."

"Oh, she's probably forgotten your size, or something," said Andy. "Or she's afraid you won't like the color."

"Mothers are like that," said Toby. The two roommates looked her way and Toby felt embarrassed. It had been so long since she'd had a mother, how would she even know?

CHAPTER FOUR

Jane was rustling through her dresser drawers, looking for her sewing kit which held a small gold-handled embroidery scissors. Under her arm was a small package tightly wrapped in brown paper and sealed with heavy tape, which had been delivered in a Federal Express bag.

"Don't wreck your scissors," said Toby. "I have an all-purpose knife that will cut through anything." She produced from her desk a folding scout knife with at least a half dozen blades, then handed it to Jane, who quickly removed the wrappings.

The outer box removed, Jane retrieved a beautiful silver-foiled box from the tissue paper. The box had a fancy pink bow, with a small envelope taped to it. When she opened the envelope she found one of her mother's panelled note cards, engraved on the front with "Mrs. David French Barrett." Inside it said:

> Happy Sixteenth Birthday
> to our dear daughter.
> Please call as soon as you
> open this.
>> Much love from
>> Mother and Father

Jane removed the bow from the package and took off the top. There lay a check for three hundred dollars, drawn on the First National Bank of Boston and signed by her father. Underneath the check, surrounded by tissue paper was a small hinged blue velvet box. As Jane made a move to open it, Andy said, "Come on, Jane! Today's not your birthday. That's cheating."

"You mean you'd expect me to sit around with a beautiful velvet box in my hand waiting until *tomorrow*?"

"It's the only honest thing to do," said Toby. "This is a birthday present. Not a day-before present."

"What if Mother had brought it to me on Sunday?" asked Jane. "I suppose then it would be a day-after present and I couldn't open it for a whole year."

Toby shrugged and said nothing. Jane's argument had her stumped.

Jane opened the hinged lid and stared in the box, which was lined with creme-colored satin. "Ohhh," she breathed. "Ohhh!"

Andy peered over her shoulder. "Pearls! Real pearls!"

Toby was not sure how one told real pearls from the ones in the dimestore. They all looked alike to her. So she said, "Oh, Jane, how beautiful!" Which they were.

A tear rolled down Jane's cheek. "These belonged to my great-grandmother Adelaide Lewis Barrett. My father's grandmother. They were her wedding gift from my great-grandfather. And with each child that was born, he added another pearl to the strand. See the five larger ones in the middle?" Jane pulled a tissue from the box on her night-stand and wiped her eyes. "Mother always told me the necklace would be mine — but I had no idea how soon! Oh, I could cry!"

"Guess what, you *are* crying," said Andy. "But I don't blame you. To think of that wedding so long ago."

"It must have been so romantic," sighed Jane.

"I can see it now. Your great-grandmother driving to the church in this lacy gown and fifty feet of veil, in a carriage drawn by four white horses with white roses around their necks."

"Wait a minute," said Toby. "How old was

your great-grandmother, anyway? The way I figure, she must have driven to the wedding in a Model T Ford."

Jane's face fell. "I guess you're right. She was married somewhere in the twenties." She shook her head. "Oh, dear. Great-grandmother Barrett in a Tin Lizzie. That kind of ruins my illusion."

"Backfiring all the way to the church," chuckled Andy.

Jane took the string of pearls in her hands, touching them gently. The necklace had a faint pink glow. "Oh, I love it, I love it!" She held the pearls to her cheek. More tears rolled down to meet them. "I'm the happiest girl in the world!"

"You sure don't look it," Andy teased, handing Jane another tissue.

Jane put on the necklace and stood in front of her bureau mirror to admire it. "They're regal, aren't they?"

"Regal?" said Toby.

"You know, like something a queen would wear."

"And the finishing touch to a T-shirt and shorts," said Andy.

"Father told me my great-grandmother rarely took them off. That's why they have such a rich patina." As she said this, the pearls slid from around her throat and dropped to the floor. "Now how did that happen?" Jane said, puzzled.

"Is the catch loose?" Andy asked.

Jane picked up the necklace from her pastel rug and examined the small oval clasp, which was studded with tiny diamonds. "Oh, I see, the fastener wasn't completely closed. See this little hook? That must be sort of a safety catch." She put the necklace on again and assumed a royal pose in front of the mirror. "Honestly, when I put these on, I feel so special. Like they're a magic charm. And when I wear them, only good things will happen."

"You're a lucky girl," said Toby, happy for Jane's good fortune but not in the least envious.

"I must call Mother right away and tell her how excited I am." She hurried out to the phones at the end of the hall and dialed Boston. But she had to leave a message with the maid. Her parents were out to dinner.

Neal arrived about half-past seven that evening. From the window of 407 Toby watched him stride across the lawn in front of Baker. Her heart began to dance a rock and roll number to a deafening beat. "He's here!" she announced to her roommates and dashed out the door and down the stairs to greet him. The pair almost collided on the steps of Baker. Toby, a little breathless, tried to look casual as she said softly, "Hi, Neal!" But when he put his arms around her she gasped with her sincere spirit, "Oh, I'm so glad to see you!"

Neal's cheek was warm against hers, and in spite of his long drive from Boston, he smelled of fresh ironing and soap. "I'm glad to see *you* Toby. *So* glad!" That was all he needed to say. Now, after months of being apart over the summer, they were again comfortable with one another.

Andy and Jane soon joined the two on the front porch of Baker and greeted Neal like he was a celebrity. "I'm so happy you could come!" said Jane. "It wouldn't seem like a birthday without you." Jane and Neal and their parents had been celebrating birthdays together since Jane was three. What Jane and Neal had once mistaken for love was actually a mutual brother-and-sister sharing, a love of a different kind, much different from the feeling he and Toby were now experiencing.

"Happy-Day-Before-Birthday," said Neal. His eyes caught the pearls at Jane's throat. "Say, aren't we fancy! That is one beautiful necklace."

"Isn't it fantastic, Neal? I'm really thrilled. You remember great-grandmother Barrett? These are her pearls. Mother sent them today as my gift."

"That's quite a present. But then, you are *sixteen* now."

"These are going to make number sixteen my best birthday ever."

Neal cocked his head thoughtfully, as if looking back into the past. "Aren't those the pearls your great-grandmother is wearing in her portrait? The one in the library. She was in a blue ballgown, I think."

"That's right! Great-grandfather commissioned that painting on her fortieth birthday. Mother had the whole room done over in that shade of blue. But I had forgotten — she *was* wearing these, wasn't she?"

"You'd better take them off and lock them up. Those pearls are too valuable to wear around."

Jane knew when Neal said this, he wasn't thinking about their worth in cash. Families like theirs had all jewelry appraised and covered by extensive insurance policies. The real value was measured in sentiment and memories — things that money couldn't replace.

"Don't worry, I'll be careful. I just wanted to wear them for a little while. To sort of break them in, you know. I haven't even been able to reach my parents to thank them."

All the time Neal was talking to Jane, he was holding Toby's hand. Andy wished she and Matt were spending the evening together. But he was busy tonight doing stock work for Greenleaf Electric, a lamp and chandelier store, where he hoped he could get steady part-time work.

"Well, gang," Andy said, "we'd better get moving. We have tons of shopping to do for the big celebration. Sorry Matt can't come along to help us."

"Cary can't help either," said Jane. "He's rehearsing, as usual."

"I'm sure the crew of 407 can get us organized," said Neal. He broke into a smile. "Just wait till you see the boat. Is she a beauty! An old classic with a wood hull."

"Are you sure all six of us — and the food — will fit?" asked Jane.

"We'll be rattling around. She's thirty-six feet with a large cabin. Parties of six sometimes charter the yawl for weekends, or even a week. That's how my friend Roger pays for his slip rental. He gave us a good price because he knows we'll take good care of everything."

Toby looked off into the distance. A luxury boat could be a big responsibility. Would the Canby threesome and their friends — who knew nothing about sailing — manage to bring it home safely? She shrugged off her doubts. After all, if Neal trusted them, why should she worry? Forcing her face into a grin, Toby said brightly, "Do we all have our grocery lists?" She pulled a folded sheet of notebook paper from the pocket of her jeans. "I took Jane at her word. I'll bet no one has an order as big as mine."

"Don't be too sure," said Jane. "I made mine up last night when I was starving."

"I didn't get around to my list," said Andy.

"So I'll just get a shopping cart and start grabbing!"

Jane ran upstairs to get the check, and minutes later the roommates were in Neal's car — a white Mercedes borrowed from his mother — on their way to the A&P. The pearls were still glowing against Jane's throat.

"Do you mind if we stop first at the bank?" asked Jane, who was sitting in the back seat, behind Neal. "I need to deposit this check at the automatic teller. Then I'll draw out cash."

"No problem," said Neal. "It's right on the way."

At the bank Jane jumped out of the car and inserted a plastic card into the computerized machine that handled her savings account. That seemed such a grown-up way of handling cash, Toby thought, instead of using, as she did, postal money orders from Rattlesnake Creek.

When Jane returned to the car, she was carrying three crisp hundred dollar bills.

"Roger gave us a special price of one hundred and fifty dollars for the day," said Neal.

"That means one hundred and fifty dollars just for food? Woweee!" said Andy. "This is going to be *some* party. We should have invited all of Baker. Or at least our floor."

"Too bad they wouldn't fit on the boat," said Jane. "But we can share the leftovers with everyone. Won't that be fun?"

"We can celebrate for days!" said Andy.

"Oh, dear," Jane sighed suddenly. "I meant to order a cake at The Upper Crust bakery. And now they're closed."

"Some sixteenth birthday committee we are," Andy said, "to forget the most important thing!"

"Well, not quite the most important," Jane said. "We're all going to be together. That's what matters most. But, of course, the birthday cake would have been the finishing touch. I was going to get German Chocolate."

"Ummm," said Andy.

"That would have been nice," said Toby. She liked her cakes in plain chocolate, but any chocolate was better than none. Maybe we can get a cake ready-made at the market."

"Yuk," said Jane. "They taste like they're a week old. With sickening flavors like Cherry Supreme or Banana Nut. There's nothing like a mouthful of rotten bananas."

"Or cherries that ooze red dye," said Neal.

"That's okay," said Andy. "We can make the cake ourselves. I know a super-special recipe that goes together in a flash."

"What kind?" asked Jane.

"That's a surprise," said Andy.

"There's even an oven on the boat?" asked Toby.

Neal chuckled as he pulled the car into the supermarket parking lot. "Do you think any modern-day sailor goes to sea without fresh-baked hard tack?"

And with that the four shoppers lined up their market carts like railroad boxcars and wheeled into the Greenleaf A&P.

"Incredible!" said Neal as he and Toby met Jane and Andy at the checkout line. Three well stocked carts stood waiting for the groceries to be rung up and bagged. The other shoppers, seeing the baskets, headed for other checkers, leaving the group alone.

"I know what we can do," said Jane. "Each of us should turn her back except when our own basket is being checked out. And Neal shouldn't watch at all. That way we can all be surprised."

"What if we all got the same things?"

"What's the difference — if we all bought our favorites. All the more for everyone." Actually Jane didn't think her roommates, especially Toby, exactly shared her tastes in food. She had stuck some smoked oysters in the basket and a jar of persimmon chutney from the Gourmet Foods section, and now she didn't want to be teased about them. After all, it was her birthday, and these *were* her favorites, even if they might seem bizarre to her roommates.

"Did you remember the birthday cake mixings?" Toby asked Andy. "I got some ice cream. Chocolate chip."

"So did I," said Andy. "Peppermint stick."

"Macadamia nut toffee," Jane chimed in.

They all laughed and Neal said, "Tomorrow I'll get some dry ice at the Ice House. I have a hunch that galley freezer will be on overload."

The tape curled out of the register like a large serpent and slithered along the floor behind the checkstand. The clerk stopped several times to give her fingers a rest. When it was their turn, each of the three girls and Neal helped the boxboy load the plastic sacks, being careful to turn their backs when purchases of the others were being bagged.

"That will be one hundred and twenty-four dollars and thirteen cents," the checker said cheerfully.

"Wow!" said Andy. "Do you think we overdid it a little?"

"Not at all," said Jane. "From the looks of it, we got our money's worth."

"*Your* money's worth," said Toby.

"We're in this together," said Jane as she handed the checker two one hundred dollar bills. "That's what makes it so perfect." She felt her neckline; the pearls were still in place.

"Have a happy birthday," said the clerk as she handed Jane the change.

As they pushed the three carts to the car, Jane turned to Andy. "Now how did that checker know?"

Andy grinned and shrugged, "Just psychic, I guess."

The shoppers left most of the grocery bags in Neal's trunk, after taking out the ice cream and perishables, which they stored in the giant refrigerator/freezer in the dining hall kitchen. Meredith Pembroke, in her TV-watching blue slippers, unlocked the kitchen for them and helped carry in the sacks. "Looks like quite a party," said Merry. "I hope all this doesn't sink the boat."

"No chance," said Neal. "The *Annabel Lee* can use the ballast." Toby wondered if Merry knew what a ballast was. Because *she* certainly didn't.

"Lock up when you're finished," said Merry, turning to leave. "And when you get upstairs, Jane, call your mother. She phoned just after you left."

"Oh, good," said Jane. "Thanks, Merry."

When the party goods were safely stored away, Toby left with Neal for the movie. But she knew they had missed the last show, and in a way she was glad. Now they could go for a ride and catch up on a summer's full of talk.

After waving good-bye, Andy and Jane locked up the kitchen and returned to 407. Andy did a few stretches, then flopped on her bed, "Say, that grocery shopping is real exercise!" she said.

"Wait till tomorrow," said Jane. "When we have to cook it."

"And more than that, eat it!" chuckled Andy. "I hope our stomachs are up to the job."

Jane went to her dresser drawer, pulled out the blue velvet box and carefully put away the pearls. Then she went down the hall and dialed home.

"Hi, Mother. Oh, yes, I am sooo excited. And so surprised! That is the most beautiful gift in the whole wide world."

There was a long pause as Mrs. Barrett cautioned her daughter to take good care of this irreplaceable gift. "Oh, don't worry, Mother. You have to know how I feel about the necklace. Why it's as precious to me as — uh — my roommates!" At this Jane's mother seemed satisfied.

"Where are the pearls now?" asked her mother.

"In their lovely box. Of course they're safe, Mother. They're in my dresser drawer."

"I want you to lock them in Meredith Pembroke's vault," came her mother's reply.

"But, Mother, you know no one at Baker would steal!"

"I'd just feel better," said her mother. "So will you promise me, please?"

"Of course. But I hate to bother Meredith."

"Well, after all, you'll only be wearing the pearls on special occasions. I want you to promise me that, too."

"Well, if you think — "

"I insist, Jane."

"Okay, I promise."

Andy could see the disturbed look on Jane's face as she put down the phone. "Mother wants me to lock up the pearls in Meredith's safe. What fun is that?"

"Well, I can see her point. After all, in a way, they belong not just to you, but to your whole family. And maybe to your children and grandchildren!"

"What a beautiful thought," said Jane.

"So, why don't we trot on over to Meredith's right now. We have to return the kitchen keys, anyway. But before we do, don't you think we should sneak a sample of tomorrow's birthday ice cream?"

"I'm for the ice cream," said Jane. "But let's skip the trip to Meredith's safe."

Andy looked shocked. "But Jane, you promised your mother. I heard you."

"I promised her I'd wear the pearls only on special occasions. And if my sixteenth birthday isn't a special occasion, I'd like to know what is!"

CHAPTER FIVE

Saturday dawned bright and clear. By eight a.m. the girls of 407 were ready for the sailing trip. They stood in front of Baker with all the birthday baggage, waiting for Neal, Cary, and Matt to pick them up in Neal's car.

The day being warm, even early in the morning, they were wearing shorts. Andy's and Jane's were white; Toby's were cut-off faded jeans, which she wore with a short-sleeved plaid shirt of light cotton. She had on her summertime cowgirl hat, shaped like the winter one, but made of finely woven straw instead of felt. Instead of the usual Western boots she wore her tennis shoes, knowing that boots and boats don't mix.

Andy was wearing running shoes and a base-ball cap. A softball, bat, and mitt lay at her feet, alongside an old stadium blanket she used to carry to Chicago football games. Jane had brought a canvas bag for bathing suits, towels, and a hair dryer along with the light windbreaker jackets that belonged to her and Andy. On top, between the straps, was Toby's leather jacket. Next to the satchel was Jane's cowhide tape case with both classic and rock selections, and next to that another case that contained a backgammon and checker set. Jane's bangs were covered by a plastic sun visor. Around her neck was a small camera in its case. And the string of pearls.

"The boys were going to make the Ice House their first stop," said Toby. "It opens at eight. So I'm sure they'll be right along." She sat on the grass and opened the sailing book.

"I wish they'd hurry," said Jane. "Before all this ice cream melts."

"Wish granted," said Andy. As if on cue, the three boys appeared from behind the trees that lined the walk between Baker and Addison. Cary was in the lead, his mirrored glasses sparkling in the sun. When he caught sight of the girls he leaped into the air, clicking this heels together. Then he dashed across the lawn to give Jane an overpowering birthday hug.

"Happy, happy, happy, happy sixteen times!" he said, picking Jane up and whirling her around.

"Ohh, Cary, take it easy," laughed Jane, breathless. "We have a long day ahead!"

Matt and Neal approached at a slower pace.

They exchanged hugs with their dates as warmly, if less vigorously, and began picking up the grocery sacks. "I feel a watermelon," said Neal.

"No fair food-guessing," said Toby. "Remember, we agreed that the whole spread is supposed to be a surprise."

"I'm not guessing, I know," said Neal. "And from the weight of it, I'd say we have a winner from the County Fair."

Cary grinned but said nothing. One of the sacks that he carried was also in the shape of a watermelon.

When they reached Neal's car, the girls found it already half loaded. Added to the groceries left in the trunk the day before, were the boys' clothes and towels, Cary's guitar, a volleyball, a Scrabble set, and a Smokey Joe portable barbecue. Matt's fishing pole hung out the window. A carton of dry ice steamed in the back seat, next to a sack of charcoal, a large portable tape player, and a plastic picnic cooler.

"Good grief!" said Cary. "Where are we going to put all this?"

"No problem where all *this* goes," said Andy "It's where do we put *us*?"

"How long is the drive?" Jane asked Neal.

"About three hours. The anchorage is expecting us around eleven."

"Dead or alive?" asked Jane. She was joking, but obviously not thrilled at the prospect of sharing her space with a car full of market bags.

Neal began packing the ice cream into the dry ice carton, while Matt and Cary rearranged the sacks. "Why don't you girls put the soft drinks in the cooler? I bought a block of ice for it. That will save us a little room."

When the car was packed as efficiently as the six could manage, there was room for three in the front seat, but only two in the back.

"Who volunteers to stay home?" asked Cary. "How about you, Jane? You got us into all this!"

A small scowl crossed her brow, under the visor. Jane didn't always go along with Cary's teasing. "Where I go, you go," she said.

"In that case, you can go in the back. And I'll squeeze between you and the cooler.

"That won't be too comfortable for you," Jane said, but her face immediately brightened.

"When I'm not happy, I'll complain," said Cary. He grinned at her and moved into the seat.

"Who else for the back?" Neal asked. "Four in the front is against he law."

Toby said nothing. She knew that Neal would want her next to him, and she had looked forward to being there, close to his muscled shoulder.

"I have an idea," said Matt. "Let's put the cooler on the floor; I can sit on that."

"I'd like everyone in a seat belt," said Neal.

After more shuffles and squeezes and crackling of bags and adjusting of seat belts, Andy ended up sharing the front seat with Toby. Matt sat in the back with the box of dry ice in his lap. Jane and Cary sat knees-in-face with their feet on the cooler. Neal called in an airline-pilot tone of voice: "Birthday Flight 16 is now ready for take-off. Please fasten seat belts and be ready to grab your oxygen masks."

Andy giggled as she pushed Matt's fishing pole out of the way. "As if we can breathe anyway!"

Five tapes later — three rock, one classical, one country — the birthday travelers caught sight of the ocean.

"I always love the first whiff of salt air," said Jane as a cool ocean breeze poured into her open window. The sea, a strip of teal the color of two of Andy's fingernails, met a pale blue horizon.

"Around the next bend is the anchorage," said Neal. As he turned the corner, he pointed, "And there she is. The *Annabel Lee*. Isn't she a beauty?"

"It's so *big*!" said Toby. "I mean, *she* is."

"Thirty-six feet," said Neal. "Think we can handle her?"

"You bet," Matt said with a confident voice. But he stared at the boat in awe.

The *Annabel Lee* had a varnished wood deck and a smooth white hull, trimmed with a maroon stripe. There were two masts, a large one to the front of the boat, a smaller one to the rear, with a windowed cabin between them.

Neal parked the car in front of the boat, got out and opened the trunk. "You can start unloading while I sign in and get the keys. Jane, I'll need the rental money."

"Right here," said Jane. Unfolding herself from the back seat, she fished in her purse. "It's here in this envelope." She fumbled and pulled out her mother's birthday note, handing it to Neal.

Neal looked into the envelope and shrugged. "This won't get us very far." He handed her back the empty envelope.

"But I was sure I put the money there. Remember when I got change at the store?" Neal shook his head.

"It has to be here." Jane looked distressed and rummaged through the bag again, pulling out a scarf and a pair of sunglasses. "Oh, wait. I was worried about losing the money. So I zipped it into the side of my tote. She reached into the side of the canvas bag and handed Neal the bills.

"Nothing like being organized," Cary teased. "Provided you write yourself notes."

"That's what happens when I try to be careful," said Jane sheepishly.

"Watch that gangplank to the dock," Neal said as he left for the anchorage office. "It looks like they just hosed it off."

The group carefully carried the gear and groceries and set them on the dock beside the boat.

By the time Neal returned, the day's supplies were waiting beside the *Annabel Lee.* "All aboard!" he said.

"What fun!" said Andy, disappearing into the cabin with Toby behind her down the wide-stepped ladder. Jane, following, tried to descend it like a stairway. Boom, she missed a step and stumbled toward her friends.

"Are you okay?" asked Toby.

"Sure," mumbled Jane. "It's so sunny out, I couldn't see down here." If "sea legs" were required for this trip, she'd be better off in the middle of the desert!

"Wow," said Toby. "A whole bunkhouse down here."

"And look," said Andy. "A mini stove and refrigerator."

"And a mini bathroom," said Jane, poking into a door marked Head.

"Isn't it beautiful?" said Andy. "And look up here. Two more mini beds."

Jane stretched herself out on one of the bunks, which had tailored plaid cushions, and turned on a tiny wall light. "Wouldn't it be wonderful," she said, her blue eyes dreamy, "if we could stay for weeks and weeks. Sail to the Caribbean Islands. Live on coconuts and bananas."

"We wouldn't need them," said Andy, going up to get a sack of groceries, as Matt and Cary handed down the first bags. "We have enough food already."

Sack after sack came down the hatch, filling the tiny galley and both bunkrooms. In order to keep a walkway clear, they began piling the groceries on the beds and on a table that folded down from the wall.

Finally Neal made his way through the plastic grocery sacks to the front end of the boat, where he opened a cabinet marked Sail Locker and drew out three large nylon sacks and some ropes.

"I don't think this is going to work," said Jane. "We can't possibly cook all this in a mini-kitchen."

"As galleys go, this is a pretty good size," said Neal. "But not big enough, I guess, for the appetites of Room 407." He put down the sail sacks and thought for a minute, then turned to a chart on the wall. "Maybe we can have a snack to tide us over. Then we'll sail up to this river." He pointed to a snaky line on the map. "There's a park and campground about five miles upstream. We can anchor and spread out a little on shore."

"Perfect," said Andy. "Meantime, let's get

a few nibbles going. I'm so hungry I could eat a horse. In fact, I think I will." She reached in one of the bags and brought out a bag of frosted animal crackers, tore it open and pulled out a pink horse.

Matt laughed. "I'm ready to pig out myself," he said and found himself a purple pig.

Andy poured some of the cookies on a plate and passed it to Toby, Jane, and Cary. Then she handed the bag to Neal. "It's feeding time at the zoo," she said. "Let the animals feed *you*." Neal laughed and took the depleted bag upstairs. Cary had meanwhile found a pan and set it on the stove to boil. "Before we get moving, I hope there's time to steam home hot dogs."

"I'll heat some buns in this cute little toaster. And chill a bowl of fruit in the refrigerator," Jane added.

Before sails were raised, the birthday cooks popped out of the hold with hot dogs and chips, cheeses and pickles and a mopping bucket filled with cold sodas.

"I think," said Matt, chomping on an oversized chip, "that I'm going to take to sailing."

"You said a mouthful," said Cary.

Lunch seemed to disappear in seconds. At a signal from Neal, "Cast off," they untied the dock hitches and the boat took off with a lurch. Jane, who was standing in the cockpit in front of Neal, suddenly found herself sitting down on the built-in deck seat, without so much as a spill from her can of strawberry soda. She cocked her head and smiled as if she'd sat down on purpose, and hoped no one had noticed that her sea legs had failed her.

CHAPTER SIX

The *Annabel Lee* sailed swiftly and smooth-ly up the coast, all three sails pulled in tight — close hauled, as Neal would say. Neal, at the tiller, from time to time checked the compass and let out the mainsheet. Matt sat behind him, ready to adjust the mizzen sail. Andy sat on the foredeck near the bow — "the pointy end" Neal had explained — in case the jib sail needed changing. Once out in the open sea the boat was able to catch the brisk northeasterly breeze and stay on course without tacking.

"So far, so good," said Neal.

"So this is sailing," said Cary. "Nothing to it." The breeze whipped his hair around his face. The portable stereo in the cockpit at his feet was playing one of his favorite group's latest.

Toby, her straw hat tied under her chin, sat on the cockpit bench next to Neal. She was itching to get her hands on the tiller. That's right, nothing to it, she thought. It's just like steering a horse. When you want the boat to go left, you push to the right. And vice versa. A couple of times Neal had called, "Coming about! Duck-o!" Then everyone ducked so they wouldn't get hit when the sails changed position. He did this when he wanted the boat to tack in the opposite direction.

As they rounded a point on the coastline, Neal issued orders to let out the sails. "Now, we're sailing with the wind abeam," he explained to Toby. "That means the breeze is blowing directly across the boom."

"I love it, I love sailing," said Toby, wishing for all the world that she could steer or drive or hold the helm or whatever it was called.

As if he read her thoughts, Neal turned to her and said, "Why don't you take over? Looks like this filly's going to behave — for a while, anyway."

Toby tried to surpress a broad grin as she took the long varnished handle in her hands. There was a lot of pull; she felt the power of the wind fighting the resistance of the sea. The bow sliced through the water, bouncing ever so slightly, like the trot of a well bred mare. She felt the rhythm; she felt at home at the helm. And she hoped Neal would notice how happy and at ease she was.

Suddenly Andy said, "I just remembered something. I'll be downstairs for a little while." She winked at Toby, and relinquished her position near the jib sail to Cary.

"Permission granted to go below," said Toby, trying her best to sound nautical.

A short while later, Jane, who had been napping on her beach towel, sat up and stretched, "I think I'll go below, too. I'm getting a bit too much sun."

"But Jane," said Toby, who had understood the meaning of Andy's wink. "Uh, wouldn't you like to sail?"

"I *am* sailing," she said tossing her head. Some strands of hair had blown into her mouth.

"I mean, would you like to steer, or something," Toby hated to give up the tiller, but she wanted to keep Jane on deck for Andy's sake.

"No, thanks," said Jane. "I think I'll stretch out on a nice, cozy bunk."

When Jane stepped down into the galley, she found Andy hard at work, whipping up a double chocolate cake, made with chocolate pudding mix for extra richness.

"Oh, shoot," Andy said. "You weren't supposed to see."

"Well, now, I saw you buying the mix at the store."

"But you didn't know what kind."

Jane wiped a batter spill off the sink with

her finger, then licked it. "Yum, how wonderful! Andy, you are such a dear, wrestling with a mini stove just for me."

"I thought this was a smooth trip," said Andy, "until I met up with a slanted kitchen floor and a bouncing mixing bowl. Look, I've sloshed all over myself!"

"Let me take over for a while."

"Make your own birthday cake? Never! That's bad luck, I think. Besides, it's your day to be a lady of leisure."

Jane didn't see anything so special about being a lady of leisure. She'd been one all her life. But, obeying Andy, she stretched out on the bunk, and put a plaid pillow behind her head, still not taking her eyes off the cake.

Andy had buttered and floured a large sheet cake pan and was now busy wrapping some small objects in aluminum foil.

"You're not supposed to be watching," said Andy.

"Try and stop me," Jane said. "It's *my* day, remember. What in the world are you doing?"

Andy dropped a small aluminum packet into the cake batter, then stirred it. "Well, okay, Miss Nosey. If you must know, I'm putting in good luck surprises. Like my mother did when we were kids. If you get a piece with the dime, you'll have wealth. If you get the key, you'll have fame. And if you get the toy ring, you'll be the first one married."

"Wonderful!" said Jane. She wondered if Cary got the toy ring — would he give it to her? But of course he would, it was her birthday. Or would he wear it himself, like he did the earring? One never knew about Cary.

Jane readjusted the pillow, freeing her hair. Such silly thoughts, she told herself. She and Cary were much too young to be serious. But, still, it was interesting to wonder about the future. It would be great if he gave her that ring. Only in fun, of course.

Matt's head appeared upside down through the hatch, just as Andy poured the batter into the pan. "Andy, could you come up for a minute? We're going to be turning, and Neal says I need you to tail the genoa sheet while I turn the jib winch."

Andy laughed. "What does *that* mean?"

"I haven't the slightest idea," said Matt. "But that's what we're going to do."

"Be right up," Andy replied. She put the cake on the sink. "Jane, could you smooth the batter a little, make sure it's even in the corners? Then put it in the oven, okay?"

After Andy left, Jane reached for a long match to light the oven. Such a bother, she thought. Why doesn't every stove have an automatic energy-saving pilot, like hers at home? She failed to notice the warning sign above the match box; Caution. Butane Gas. She opened the oven door, found a hole in the oven floor saying Light oven here. She turned on the gas, struck the match and stuck it down the hole. Boom! She felt a hot breath of flame as the butane exploded, throwing her back on the bunk.

Her heart racing, she stared at the oven. It was heating now, just like normal ovens. She felt her eyebrows and eyelashes. They were still there, thank goodness; the flame hadn't singed them. Silly girl, she reprimanded herself. Good thing no one sees you cowering before a kitchen stove. She pulled herself up a bit shakily, took the spatula off the counter and began smoothing the cake.

With the spatula blade she fished through the batter to see where the toy ring had landed. When she found it, she pushed it into the center where she could easily find it when she cut the cake. Then she could arrange to give that piece to Cary. She smoothed the cake again, then carried it to the oven.

"Ready about hard alec," she heard Toby call. She braced herself with the cake in her arms. The boat gave a wild lurch, there was a violent flapping of sails, then a shout and splash.

"Man overboard!" called Neal. "Cary, you okay? Matt, pull in the jib. No, keep it on the port side. Cary, stay where you are. We'll circle, I'll throw you a line off the starboard."

"Oh, Cary!" Jane whispered, clutching the

cakepan. The boat lurched again. And Jane found herself with her face in the batter.

Jane ran to the head and peered out the window. Cary was treading water, holding the line Neal had thrown to him. He was fine, in fact he was laughing so hard he was swallowing water. But, in the head mirror Jane saw that she was not so fine. She looked like something from one of those old time pie-throwing comedies, the blue eyes peering through a mask of chocolate. She wished she could laugh at herself like Cary. But she was too embarrassed. Why hadn't she put the cake in the oven instead of fishing around for that silly ring?

Jane still had the cake in her arms. She heard Neal call "Coming about!" again; this time she held on tight, bracing herself against the wall. More laughter from above as Neal hauled Cary aboard. She should be up there. But how could she let them know about this latest slip — or was it slop?

The answer was simple. She couldn't.

Returning to the galley, Jane smoothed the imprint of her nose from the batter, then put the cake in the oven. The oven shelf had little clamps on it, to keep the pan from sliding. Then she went back to the head, soaked the end of a towel in cold water and mopped her face clean. The batter was even in her bangs.

From the canvas bag she brought out her swimsuit. She stripped off the chocolately T-shirt, rinsed it out in the tiny sink below the medicine chest and tossed it in a cabinet underneath. Before Jane went upstairs, she put a pink terrycloth coverup over her bathing suit and covered her damp bangs with a pink scarf.

As she emerged from the cabin, she decided if she played it cool, no one would even know about Jane Klutz Barrett, Miss Cake-in-the-Face.

Cary was drying himself with the towel Jane had left on deck. "Hey, where have you been?" he called. "You missed all the fun!"

"Oh, too bad! I saw out the window you were taking a swim, so I put on my suit to join you." Not wanting to look Cary in the eye, she looked down at the water. "How was it?"

"A mite chilly, I'd say. Sorry, I don't think I'll be taking another dip for a while."

"Well, in that case," said Jane. "I won't either." She could feel herself relax. She'd gotten away with it. And she didn't even have to get wet.

"We had a small accident," Neal explained. "A sudden shift in the wind. The mizzen boom knocked Cary overboard."

"Oh, Cary!" said Jane, all concerned. "I'm so glad you're all right. You might have drowned!" She glanced over at Toby and wished she could swallow those words. Toby was no longer at the helm. And one look at her downcast expression told Jane her Texas roommate felt like *she* was the one who was the klutz.

CHAPTER SEVEN

As they sailed up the river, Neal had Cary and Toby loosen the smaller sails, while he let the wind fill the mainsheet. The strong breezes subsided as the boat meandered up the river.

"This is nice," said Matt. "Quiet and peaceful. Just like I pictured it."

Toby had to agree with him. After the boat had bucked on her like an unbroken stallion she wanted nothing more to do with unpredictable winds. At least until she knew more.

For Neal the winds seemed to hold no surprises. He must have known that the turn into the river would be tricky. He had reached for the helm and said, "Better let me take over." But like a greenhorn, Toby had said, "I've got it, I'm fine!" just seconds before poor Cary was knocked into the water.

Everyone had tried to make a joke of it. But

Cary could have been seriously hurt. Maybe suffered a concussion. Even been knocked unconscious and drowned.

Toby was angry with herself. Why did she always try to do more than she was able? Like riding the toughest horse. Challenging the best tennis players. Acting boldly confident when she was shaking inside. Was she a born show-off? And how Toby hated show-offs.

Neal took his attention from the billowing sail and turned to Toby. "Why so solemn?"

Toby forced a smile. "Solemn, who me?"

"Tell me," Neal said softly. "What's the matter?"

"Nothing, nothing, really," Toby insisted. "Uh, I'm just hungry, I guess," she fibbed.

Neal laughed. "I could have sworn we ate less than an hour ago."

Toby did not answer. She knew Neal could see right through her. That was the beautiful part of their friendship. He could almost read her thoughts. He had to know how stupid she felt about her wild turn.

Up on the front deck Jane sat with Cary, Matt, and Andy. Cary had brought out his guitar and was tuning it. "We should get a picture of this," said Toby, trying to take the attention away from herself. "Jane, where's the camera?"

"Let's see," Jane said. "I took it off when I was lying on my towel up here. Is it in the cockpit?"

Neal moved a few life preserver cushions. "Not here," he said.

"Toby, can you peek downstairs?" asked Jane.

Toby did more than peek, she went down the ladder and searched the cabin. No camera.

"Not there," she called to Jane. And as she looked at Jane's puzzled face, Toby had a sudden realization. When she had blundered, bringing the boat suddenly about, the camera had probably slid into the water.

"Oh, well," said Jane, seeming unconcerned. "I'm sure it will turn up when we unload for shore."

Cary broke into a song, "River Rat Rock," and for the moment the camera was forgotten by everyone but Toby. She lapsed into silence again.

Neal's voice roused her from her gloom. "You're still worried that you blew it on that turn?"

"Well I did, didn't I?"

"Not at all. In fact, for a beginner you did very well. A jibe is a very difficult maneuver."

"A jibe?"

"That's when you push out on the tiller, instead of bringing it toward you. We lost control because the sails were full."

"I did it all wrong," said Toby, biting her lip.

"Coming about hard alee, means pulling the tiller toward the boom. That's the opposite of a jibe. So I wasn't quite prepared for the shift. But it was a difficult turn, no matter what. You did fine. Except, maybe, for the language."

Toby felt like crawling into a dark corner of the galley. Why did she have to act so smart, spouting off memorized nautical terms when she didn't know their meaning? On a ranch that kind of a person would be called a dude.

"You have the makings of a real sailor," Neal went on. "You seem to have a feel for the wind. That's what counts." Then he took her hand and put it on the tiller, under his.

Toby looked up at Neal and smiled, picturing the two of them racing at Newport. Accepting a trophy at the yacht club dance, taking it out on the veranda to admire it in the moonlight, he in a summer blazer, she in a lacey dress. She was speechless. But Cary's strumming filled in for her silence.

"And now, matey," Neal was saying, "could you start bringing down the mainsail? We're pulling in at the campground dock just ahead."

Toby untied the halyard and slowly let down the mainsheet. As she did, a sweet odor arose from the cabin. Dark chocolate. "Say, Andy," she called, "did you forget something?" she called.

"The cake!" said Andy. "Holy Chicago, I'll bet it's burned to an ash."

CHAPTER EIGHT

Like ants carrying crumbs of bread, the group toted the supplies from the dock to a picnic table on a high ledge overlooking the river, which moved lazily in the afternoon sun. The banks were lined with sycamores, their green turning to red and gold. Below was a sandy beach with a volleyball court, but there was no net. At the crest of the canyon, they could see the roofs of several mobile homes. But no campers were visible, except a white-haired fisherman, who stood casting from the shore into the river.

"Can't park your boat there," he said. Neal looked at the sign on the dock. For passenger loading and unloading only. No diving.

"But there's nobody here," Cary protested.

"The ranger will be around soon enough," said the man, who was round and red-faced. His reel spun, the weight splashed in the water.

"So now what do we do?" asked Jane. She was still panting from five trips up to the picnic table. "Load up and leave?"

"No way," said Neal. "This is perfect. There's nothing like a picnic in the fall, when the campgrounds are almost empty."

"But the boat," Matt said. "You can't leave it there."

"I'll anchor it on the other side of the river," Neal said, "and swim back. The river's still warm this time of year." He headed for the boat.

"Want some help?" Toby asked and followed Neal to the dock.

"I'm still wet," Cary said. "Might as well take another swim myself." He and Neal stripped off their shirts and dropped them on the dock float. "Come on, Jane," Cary said. "You said you were ready for a swim." Jane had no choice but to leave her terry coverup on the dock and follow him onto the boat.

"Matt and I will stay here and guard the picnic," Andy suggested.

"There's no one in the campground anyway," Jane said. "And I'm sure this man — what did you say your name was, sir?"

"Henry," said the fisherman.

"I'm sure Henry will look after our belongings," Jane finished. If she was going to have to swim the river on her special day, *everyone* was going to join her. "Come on Andy and Matt," she called, "We're all in this together!"

When the boat was safely anchored across the river and out of the current, Jane called, "Last one in is a rotten banana," then jumped into the water holding her nose. She was followed by her roommates, who hadn't bothered to change into their swimsuits. The birthday revelers swam back to the campground, laughing and water-fighting all the way. Neal followed at a safe distance from the splash, doing a side-stroke with one hand. In his other hand he held up the pan with the birthday cake; Andy had left it cooling on the galley sink. It had not burned. Now it must not be drowned.

The birthday feast was finally over. The sun shone from behind the hill on the far side of the river, casting its glow on the trees along the riverbank. The camp fire shed the same glow on the group's contented faces as they toasted marshmallows for S'mores, the graham cracker/chocolate/marshmallow treat Toby had learned in 4-H. But no one was eating. At this point the sight of food was almost revolting. The girls had decided to make the S'mores and take them back to their friends at Baker. Maybe they could warm them up with their hair-dryers.

"Well, I must say," said Henry, "I haven't had such a meal in a month of Sundays." He patted his wide belly with satisfaction.

"I've never tasted better trout," said Jane. "You were so kind to share with us."

"Catfish," said Henry. "And the pleasure was all mine." He stroked his small white goatee. "Never cleaned a fish in my life," said Henry. "And never intend to. Ever since I lost my missus, I just throw 'em back in."

Andy winced. Even after Henry's coaching, Matt had not been able to pull in a fish. So Henry, with four fresh fish in his creel, offered to give the group all his catch, provided *they* do the cleaning. Matt and Andy, at a nearby picnic table, cleaned the fish according to Henry's instructions while the rest of the group lit the charcoal in the portable barbecue and built a fire beneath the larger campground grill.

After working in her father's restaurant in Chicago, Andy was used to the smell of raw fish, but she had never had to cook or clean them. Her father's restaurant for the most part catered to meat-eaters. But she went along with Matt's enthusiasm, held her breath, and did her job. And the result, seared over charcoal topped with Jane's almond butter, had been well worth the work.

The rest of the feast had been equally tempting. Toby barbecued steaks medium rare. Jane added sautéed sliced mushrooms by wrapping them in foil with pats of butter.

Toby barbecued ears of corn in their husks over the coals.

Matt punched holes in the potatoes, wrapped them in foil, and put them over the coals.

Andy made a fruit salad and a gigantic lettuce bowl with three kinds of dressing. Then she opened a can of ready-made frosting and spread it on the cake, topping it with chocolate sprinkles that reminded her of ants.

Jane put out a pasta salad and an antipasto salad from the store's deli section; also two frozen pizzas, which she wrapped in foil and put on the barbecue to heat; some brie and pate; some smoked oysters and English crackers, which everyone nibbled at before they dove into the cheese puffs (Andy); popcorn (Toby); and peanut butter on celery (Neal). Cary buttered three loaves of French bread, and at Jane's request, put Parmesan on one.

There were also assorted treats that no one admitted to buying, and the two heavy watermelons.

"I vote for a watermelon eating contest," said Andy.

"How about a seed spitting contest?" Toby added.

"Great idea!" said Cary, holding his ribs. "How about a week from Tuesday?"

"I want to die," said Jane. "Absolutely die."

"Of happiness?" asked Cary.

"Of fullness," said Jane. "Uh, well, of happiness, too."

Cary reached into his guitar case and pulled

out a small package and set it on the table next to the cake.

"Oh, Cary, how nice!" said Jane. "But don't you remember? I said 'No gifts.' "

"Just a little memento — for a very big occasion."

Jane pulled off the white tissue paper, revealing a cassette tape. But there was no label on it to tell the name of the song or the artist. She looked at it, puzzled. "But who. . . ."

In answer Cary took the tape and put it in the cassette player. Jane covered her face as the band began to play. It was Ambulance, with Cary leading on guitar and singing,

> Hey Jane, Jane, Jane.
> What's this game we're playin'?
> How come you're not sayin'
> What you really mean?

"Oh, Cary!" Jane giggled, blushing. She threw her arms around him in a big hug. "What a great idea," said Andy. She and Toby remembered when, a year ago, Cary had brought all of Baker to the windows with this serenade, trying to get Jane to go out with him.

"I figured it had to be a great song," Cary said as the music played on, "to win out with a hardnose like you. So I finally polished it up and taped it. I'm sending it around to schools along with a letter asking for an audition."

"Great idea," said Matt. "I like the tune a lot."

"An inspired work, you might call it," Cary replied.

Jane, still speechless, gave Cary another hug. "I am one lucky girl," she said finally, "to have my own special composition by the soon-to-be-world famous Ambulance!"

"To success," said Neal, raising a root beer. Who would have thought that when this song was composed, he and Cary were rivals?

Neal reached into the pocket of his jacket and pulled out a small package. "As you said, 'No gifts,' so this is just a remembrance — to help you remember."

In it was a picture frame. "Oh, Neal, that's wonderful," said Jane. "I'll frame our favorite picture of the day. Then we can keep the big sixteen with us always." She turned to the group. "By the way, did anyone find the camera?"

"I did," said Matt. "It was in one of the grocery bags, of all places. Underneath the cookies."

Jane said nothing. She had no explanation. Sometimes these things just happened. Toby had gone to the satchel and brought back two more wrapped packages. "Two more non-gifts," she said. "This lumpy one's from me."

"The other is from Matt and me," said Andy. "Something else to help you remember."

"A journal," said Jane, opening Andy's polka-dotted wrappings. The book was polka-dotted, too. "Terrific! And look, it has its own pen inside."

"A special journal," said Andy. "You are now the official scribe of 407, charged with the duty of recording in detail all the goings on in Baker."

"So that none of us will ever forget a single minute," Toby said.

"Oh, I only wish I could," said Jane. "Remember, I mean. I wish my memory were good enough."

"You don't need a good memory if you put things down every day," said Andy.

Toby handed Jane the lumpy package. Inside was a tiny prickly pear cactus. "Why, Toby, how wonderful!" Jane said.

"You'd better like it, because you're stuck with it," chuckled Toby.

"I love it. What a great reminder of Texas, And you."

"And you don't have to remember to water it," said Toby.

"Thank you all so much," said Jane. She sounded almost teary. "With or without reminders, there's no way I could forget a moment of this day."

Andy picked up the camera and started snapping pictures.

"I guess now it's time for ice cream and cake," said Toby. "We have strawberry and pineapple toppings, besides the nuts and whipped cream."

"Ohhh!" sighed Jane. "How nice." She sighed again. "Can we save it till later though?"

"But we have to sing the birthday song, blow out candles, and make wishes," said Andy. "You can't be a birthday dropout!"

Jane bent wearily over the picnic table to comply with the request. She made a wish — that all her birthdays could be spent with such good friends. She blew the candles out, but just barely. Her stomach was beginning to hurt.

"A toast to the birthday girl," said Andy. "To sixteen!"

"To sixteen!" echoed the group, raising soda cans.

"Let's get a picture of all of us together," said Andy. "Henry, could you . . . Henry?"

Henry did not answer. He was dozing soundly under a tree, his hat as a pillow against the trunk. "Uh, well maybe later," said Andy, and she snapped a picture of the sleeping figure.

Toby dished out three flavors of ice cream as Jane served the cake.

"Just a sliver," begged Andy.

"Same for me," said Neal.

Cutting slices so narrow, there was no way that Jane could reach the ring in the middle of the cake. Nor did she care. At this point all she wanted was to lie down for a big fat nap, because big and fat was how she felt. "Along with our friend Henry, I vote for a *siesta*," she said.

No one raised a voice to disagree.

Neal jostled the nappers back to life. "We'd better get moving."

The girls were curled up by the fire on Andy's stadium blanket. The three boys had rolled up their jackets as pillows, each taking a picnic bench as a bed. Henry the fisherman had disappeared.

Jane sat up and stretched. "If I could have just one more birthday wish, I'd ask that I could sleep a couple more hours."

"You can sleep on the boat," said Neal. "We want to get back before dark. The wind starts to die down at sunset."

The girls quickly packed the remains of the birthday feast. Cary and Matt cleaned up the campsite, doused the fire, and carried the supplies to the dock while Neal swam to the boat and brought it back.

When everyone was on board, Jane breathed a wistful sigh as she looked at the sky, now full of rosy sunset clouds. "I am going to hate to see this day end. Thank you all for being with me. It was the best birthday of my life. Really. A very special occasion."

As if to underline her words, she reached for her pearls.

Her throat was bare.

CHAPTER NINE

Jane lay on one of the boat bunks, sobbing into a pillow. "Oh, it can't be, it can't be. Tell me this is a nightmare!"

"Don't worry, Jane," said Toby. "The pearls are sure to turn up somewhere." But her voice did not sound convincing.

Cary, Matt, and Toby had made a thorough search of the shore and the campground while the rest had poked into every nook and cranny of the boat — opened all drawers, overturned cushions, felt into the cracks behind the bunks. Andy even looked in the refrigerator.

"There's still the car to search," Andy said brightly. "And even our room. We may find your pearls in the dresser drawer."

"No chance," said Jane with a sniff. "I remember. When I put the camera around my neck, I made sure the strap didn't rub against the necklace clasp."

"Do you remember feeling the pearls after

that?" asked Andy. "Like when you put the camera in the cookie bag?"

"I took off the camera when I was on deck," Jane insisted. "I don't know who put it in the groceries."

Toby had been much relieved when the camera was found — her clumsy handling of the boat had not thrown the camera into the water. And certainly not into the sack filled with Oreos. But what about the pearls? From anywhere on the foredeck, they could have easily slid into the sea. On the other hand, if Jane didn't remember bringing the camera into the cabin, she might also have slipped off the pearls and stashed them someplace without thinking. Toby got off the bunk and checked the head again, this time in the medicine chest and under the sink. She found Jane's damp T-shirt.

Jane was still wearing her bathing suit, which had now dried, and her pink terry coverup. Toby and Andy had gone to the campground washroom to put on their dry swimsuits after dinner, letting their wet shorts and shirts hang by the fire while they napped. In the boat's cabin they had changed back into their shorts for the trip home.

"Jane, isn't this shirt yours?" asked Toby, holding up her discovery.

"Uh, yes," said Jane. "I got a little smudge of chocolate on it while I was putting the cake in the oven." She tried to remember if she was still wearing the pearls when she changed into her swimsuit. But all she could think of was her face full of chocolate cake mess.

No doubt about it, her pearls were at the bottom of the ocean. Or the bay. Or the river. Unless . . . A terrible thought came to mind.

"Toby. Andy. What did you think of that fisherman? Henry."

"Nice man," said Toby.

"Very nice," said Andy. "But sort of lonely. What's that got to do with anything?" Andy looked down at her hands. She had scrubbed them twice and still felt they smelled of fish.

"He left while we were asleep," said Jane. "You don't suppose. . . ."

Toby gasped, "That he took your pearls? Oh, no. That couldn't be. He was a dear old man."

"Yes, I'll bet that's it," said Jane. She felt her knotted stomach relax. It felt better, somehow, to think the pearls were stolen. It was easier to give up hope, rather than to keep searching and hating herself for being so careless. "Henry," she said, "That's got to be it."

She got up, took the wet T-shirt, and hung it on a mini hanger in the mini closet to dry. Then, wiping the last tear from her face, she straightened herself and climbed up the ladder to the deck. "Henry," she said to herself. "I wish that awful man would grow a giant wart on his nose."

Toby and Andy abandoned the cabin search

and followed their roommate up the ladder. Henry, thought Andy. It could be. That's why city girls were always taught not to get friendly with strangers. Maybe the same rules applied in the country. And then the thought struck her. By pure chance she had snapped a picture of this man, asleep under the tree.

The boat was now at the mouth of the river, drifting into the ocean. Drifting is right, thought Toby. The mainsail was pulled in tight but still flapping. The boat's only forward movement was caused by the river current.

"I was afraid of this," Neal said. "The wind's gone."

"Can't we turn around and sail backward?" asked Andy.

Toby laughed. "Hey, there's an idea!"

"Looks like our luck changed with the wind," said Jane, her face glum. To think that less than an hour ago she had thought this the happiest day of her life.

"Not to worry," said Neal. "I'll start the engine. If we pull out a little from shore, we may pick up a breeze."

"Well, of course," said Jane, brightening. "I forgot we had an engine." At this point she was ready to motor all the way back to get the day over with. Or was she? When Jane got home, she should call her mother at once and tell her about the loss. She cringed at the thought. No, better they stay at sea.

Neal took the boat keys and inserted them in the dashboard next to the compass. He turned the key and the motor whined, then stopped. He looked puzzled, then tried again. This time there was a click, then silence.

"Problems?" asked Cary.

"Problems," said Neal. "A dead battery."

"Oh, no!" wailed Jane. "What more can happen?"

"So, now what?" asked Matt.

"We have a couple of choices. We can either drift out to sea, or drift into shore."

"Can't we drop anchor?" asked Toby, trying to be helpful. Drifting seemed so out of control.

"We can *drag* anchor," said Neal. "The water here is about two hundred fathoms. That would slow us down a little. But I for one would like to get either into the wind or onto shore. If we drift to land, I can call the Coast Guard for help."

He shook his head. "I should have thought to check the battery. Some captain I am."

Toby felt sorry for Neal. He was such a confident sailor, a racing expert who had won dozens of trophies. Now he was feeling just like Toby had felt earlier. She found herself hoping that there was something seriously wrong with the engine, not just a dead battery.

"Meanwhile," said Neal, "we might as well enjoy ourselves."

"Sure," said Andy, trying to put some cheer into the group. "Enjoy the moment!" She turned up Cary's stereo that, oddly enough, was playing Haydn's water music. (Jane's choice.) She looked at the glum faces around her. This was a lot harder than when she was a junior high school cheerleader in Chicago. "Jane, remember what you said earlier?" Andy said. "About wanting to stay here for days and days? Wish granted. Let's be happy!"

"Oh, my!" said Jane. She clapped her hand over her mouth, covering a horrified expression. "After this I'd better be careful about what I wish!"

"Maybe it's magic," said Toby. "Like on this special day — sixteenth birthday on the sixteenth day of September — everything you wish for comes true."

Jane looked panic-stricken. "Oh, dear. What else have I wished for today?" Her thoughts raced through the day. She'd wished the boys would hurry so the ice cream wouldn't melt. And that she wasn't such a klutz. And that all her birthdays would be spent with such good friends. So far so good. But then there was that other wish. That Henry, who had probably stolen her pearls, would grow a gigantic wart on his nose. Should she take it back? *Could* she?

Jane pictured Henry's nose. A lonely old man who'd lost his wife. Now — if the wart grew big enough — he might lose his friends, too. "I'll take it back," she muttered.

"Take what back?" said Andy.

"Oh, nothing, nothing," Jane spluttered. "I was just thinking about the scarf my Aunt Priscilla sent me last week for my birthday. It doesn't match anything." Jane had an Aunt Priscilla. But she hadn't seen or heard from her since last year's family reunion. I wish I could stop fibbing, she thought.

"COXSWAIN," Neal announced as he spelled it out on the Scrabble board. "With the X on the triple word score that's a total of sixty points! And I'm out of the game."

"Booo!" said Cary.

"Anyone for another game?" said Neal. By a flickering candle he rechecked his tally as if he were going to be paid in cash.

"Sure," said Toby. She was happy to see Neal in good spirits again.

"I knew that a couple of games would come in handy," said Matt, "even if I didn't know why."

The group sat around the fold-down table in the boat cabin, two dripping candles on saucers their only light. With no battery power, the cabin lamps would not light. A bowl of popcorn sat beside the Scrabble board, and each player had a fresh cold soda. Jane was stretched out on an upper bunk, watching the players, but not participating. She was lying there wishing. Wishing with all her heart that they could get back home. That Meredith Pembroke wouldn't punish them for being out after hours. And that the pearls would, by some miracle, turn up.

The Barretts would be coming for her birthday dinner the next day. Jane had planned to wear her blue linen dress with the scooped neck. Did she have a turtle necked outfit to cover up? Only that scratchy gray wool jersey. With the weather in the high seventies, her mother would think she'd lost her mind.

Cary dropped out of the game and began picking at his guitar.

Neal periodically left the Scrabble board to peer out of the hatch, checking how near they were to shore. But so far the white lights that lined the coast were growing dimmer. The rudder and sails were tied in place. And the mainsail, pulled in tight, continued to flutter in powerless puffs of wind. Neal had attached an emergency flashlight to the boom to attract help.

Toby looked at Neal's waterproof watch. Ten-thirty p.m. It was a three-hour trip back to Greenleaf. Even if they landed this minute they couldn't get in by the one a.m. lockup at Canby Hall. How would Meredith Pembroke take the old "dead battery" excuse, even if it was a boat instead of a car? What a great way to start the year, being confined to Baker for who knows how many weekends!

Cary strummed a few wistful chords on the guitar. The boys were signed out until two a.m. If they didn't get back, he'd be confined to campus next weekend. He'd miss his chance to play at Hillsboro. And after that? What prep school would trust Ambulance after they'd pulled a no-show at Hillsboro Homecoming?

Being confined to 407 meant that Andy couldn't get to tryouts next weekend for the Christmas performance of "Nutcracker." But she was determined to keep smiling, to keep nibbling popcorn as if she were enjoying herself. "Look here!" she said, with a smile. "*Catastrophy* for thirty-eight points." She added *catas* to the *trophy* Neal had spelled out for his last turn.

"Sorry," said Neal. "I challenge. It's spelled *c-a-t-a-s-t-r-o-p-h-e.*"

Jane felt resentful of all the smiles and giggles. Her friends were acting as if this were another picnic. Didn't they even care? "Ohhh!" she wailed, her face contorted with impatience. "I wish, I wish something would happen!"

And at that very moment the boat began to rock. Cary stopped strumming his guitar. Neal sat up and listened. There was the roar of a motor approaching and the splash of its wake as it circled the sailboat. A voice shouted "Coast Guard here!"

"Wish granted, my friend," said Andy.

CHAPTER TEN

Y ou're safe, that's all that counts," said Meredith. She poured the girls each a cup of warm chocolate. The clock said two-thirty a.m., but no one was sleepy now. The girls had dozed on the car trip home, too weary to talk about their rescue by the Coast Guard. But now they were anxious to fill Meredith in on the details of their day, as they stored the remains of the party in her refrigerator.

"It's weird," said Toby. "All last week I worried that we'd get caught in a terrible storm and not know what to do. And as it turned out, we were trapped in a terrible calm."

"And we still didn't know what to do," said Andy.

"Seems to me you two did just right," said Jane. "You kept calm in the calm. Instead of acting all stormy like I did."

"So anyway," Toby continued, "it turned

90

out to be a simple problem. The Coast Guard men attached some thingeys to the whatsits on the battery, and we were off in a flash."

"The Coast Guard is wonderful," said Meredith. "They were so polite and nice. And so concerned. I'm so happy I thought to call them."

Jane's mouth dropped open. "You called them? About us? Meredith, are you psychic? How did you know we were in trouble?"

Meredith looked down at her blue fuzzy slippers. "Well, when it got dark and I hadn't heard from you I started worrying that maybe there was a storm or something. So I called the weather forecast number and they said there was a flat sea with winds 0 to 1 mile an hour. So then I couldn't figure out what had happened, or why you hadn't called. And that's what I told the man at the Coast Guard. Dooley, his name was. Mr. Dooley."

"You were expecting us to call?" Andy asked.

"Why, yes," said Meredith. "Don't you remember, Jane? You told me Friday night you'd have so much food left over, why didn't we have a party for the girls on your floor. You were going to call me when your boat returned to shore."

"Oh, my goodness," said Jane. "So I did. With all the, uh, problems I completely forgot the party.

"Dee and Maggie were so disappointed.

They'd nearly popped their lungs blowing up balloons." Dee Adams and Maggie Morrison roomed next door in 409 and were close friends of their 407 neighbors.

"Ohhh!" Andy said.

"I'm sorry!" said Toby, even though it wasn't her fault.

"Well, never you mind," said Meredith. "If I hadn't expected to hear from you, that boat might still be drifting." She stood and gathered up the cups, taking them to the sink. "The party will keep until tomorrow. In the meantime, we all need a good rest."

Back in her room Jane lay awake, listening to the heavy breathing of her roommates, who had dropped off to sleep immediately. Her bed felt as if it were bobbing, as if Jane were still on the bunk of the sailboat. She kept picturing the loving faces of her parents at the dinner table Sunday evening, particularly her mother's puzzled look as she asked, "But, Jane, dear, why aren't you wearing your pearls?"

How could she find the courage to tell them the truth? She hadn't even been able to tell Meredith about her loss.

She turned over in bed and punched her down pillow. "Oh, I wish I weren't such a chicken," she sighed to herself. The faint tick tick of her quartz clock reminded Jane that it was long after midnight. Maybe birthday wishes all came true. But it was no longer her birthday.

CHAPTER ELEVEN

B ut, Jane, you've got to tell your parents. You've got to!" said Toby.

"No matter how much it hurts," said Andy.

Jane was sitting up in bed, her arms wrapped around her knees, which were still under the quilt. The Sunday morning sun was bright outside the window; the girls had slept late after their much-delayed bedtime.

Jane put her hands to her temples, as if trying to wipe out a headache. "You just don't understand my mother," she said.

"What about your father?" asked Andy. "After all, the pearls came from *his* grandmother. He deserves to know that you've lost them."

Jane sighed. How she wished her parents hadn't trusted her with the pearls, a responsibility to which she clearly was not equal. "It's not that I'm *not* going to tell them. I'm just not going to tell them *now*."

"What's the difference?" asked Toby. She straightened her bed and pulled on a pair of jeans. In a few minutes Neal would be by to go riding at Randy Crowell's ranch — if he, too, hadn't overslept.

The phone rang by Jane's bed. "That's probably Neal," Toby said as Jane picked up the receiver. She saw her roommate's face turn ashen.

"Oh, Mother!" said Jane. "I didn't expect to hear from you so early. Where are you?"

"We're in Countrywood," Mrs. Barrett answered. "Actually, we left Boston yesterday morning," she said. "We decided to make a little vacation of our visit. We've been taking the side roads and enjoying the fall foliage. The travel agent found us this lovely country inn. A bed and breakfast, actually. Furnished with the most exquisite antiques."

"That's nice," said Jane, trying to sound enthusiastic.

"How was your birthday?" her mother asked.

"Oh. Oh, it was lovely, of course. We went sailing all day. Had a picnic. Yes, it was perfect." She felt her stomach knot as she said the words.

"Countrywood is only seventy-five miles from Greenleaf," Gloria Barrett said. "So we thought we might have lunch with you and spend the afternoon — as well as having dinner."

"Uh, oh, wonderful!" said Jane, but her voice belied her enthusiasm.

"I mean, of course, if you don't have plans."

"Plans? No. No plans," said Jane. Except to search Neal's car again. And the room. And call the anchorage to see if the pearls had been found on the dock. "I mean, that's great," said Jane.

"Are you all right?" asked Gloria.

"Fine, just fine."

"You sound as if you ate too much birthday cake," said her mother.

"Hardly that!" Jane thought about the cake in Meredith's refrigerator, barely touched. And right now she felt as if she would never want to eat again. The lump in the pit of her stomach was that heavy.

"Well, we'll look forward to lunch," said her mother. "To tell you the truth, the breakfast was only a stale cheese danish and instant coffee. But it was served on lovely Limoges china."

"Lunch," said Jane, absently. "That will be fine."

"I'll call you as soon as we check in."

"Fine, Mother."

"Jane, please stop saying 'fine.' You always use that word when something's wrong."

"I'm fine, Mother. I mean — everything's wonderful. Really."

"Why don't you ask Cary to join us for

lunch?" her mother asked. "And your room-mates, too, if they're free."

"Oh, too bad. Cary has to work today," said Jane. Inwardly she was delighted that Cary had traded his Saturday shift for Sunday. She knew also that Cary would not be terribly excited about having lunch or dinner with the Barretts, who were part of the Boston society of his parents.

"I'm sorry," Mrs. Barrett said. "I had looked forward to seeing Cary." She paused, while Jane rolled her eyes toward the ceiling in relief. "Say, I have an idea," her mother went on. "Why don't we have lunch at Cary's diner? I think that would be fun. You know your father loves hamburgers. And this week-end, in honor of your birthday, he's off his diet."

"Great!" said Jane, who didn't dare say fine again, which *was* what she said when things weren't fine at all. Her mother sometimes understood her much too well.

"Cary! Did I get you up!"

"Oh, hi, Jane," Cary said into the telephone, his eyes still closed. "What's up? I mean, besides you?"

"Oh, I'm sorry," Jane said. "I thought you'd be awake! Your shift at the diner begins in an hour."

"I allow myself fifteen minutes," Cary mumbled. "That's if I want to shower."

"I'm sorry to disturb you," said Jane. "But you'd better be forewarned. My parents are coming to lunch. At the Greaf."

"Good greaf!" said Cary. Then, catching himself, he said "Fine! Thanks for the tip. I'll wipe the mustard off my shirt. Do you want me to take off my earring, too?"

"I know you'd never do that. Not even when waiting on the Barretts of Boston."

"*Especially* not for the Barretts of Boston," he said. People like his parents and the Barretts were the reason he wore the earring in the first place.

"I want to remind you," said Jane, "about the pearls. Don't let on that they're lost."

"But, Jane," Cary said flatly. "They *are*."

"They're not lost. Just misplaced," she said. "Or maybe stolen by that dreadful Henry. The pearls are safe someplace. I just don't at this moment know where."

"So what are you going to tell your parents?" asked Cary. "I mean, what's the script, so I don't blow my lines?"

Jane paused, tapping the phone receiver with her clear-polished fingernail.

"I'm not sure what I'm going to tell them. Or what I'm going to do. Probably stall for time. Because I *know* the pearls will turn up."

"You weren't that sure yesterday," said Cary.

"Well, anyway," said Jane. "Whatever's

happening, I want to know you'll go along with me."

Cary sighed. "Sure. I'll be cool. But don't think that means I approve of what you're doing."

"Why not?" asked Jane in an almost shrill voice.

"Because you're being dishonest."

"I'm just trying to keep my folks from worrying."

"They've been worrying about you since the first time you fell out of your stroller. Why spare them now?"

"Because now I'm grown up," said Jane.

"Oh," said Cary. Dead silence followed.

"What do you mean, 'Oh.'?" Jane asked.

"You know very well what I mean. Being grown up means taking responsibility for your mistakes. Owning up to them. How else can you promise yourself you'll be smarter next time?"

"I *will* be smarter next time," Jane said.

"But in the meantime, you're not tough enough to face the music," Cary said.

"Sure. I could face the music. But you know my parents. Their music and ours just isn't the same."

"When it comes to honesty," Cary said, "there's only one tune."

"So where does that leave us?" Jane asked, raising her voice frantically.

"Don't worry, my dear sweet-sixteen. I

I won't serve up the burgers with a side of spilled beans."

"Thanks," Jane said. "I knew I could count on you."

"Sure," Cary replied. "And I hope I can do the same."

"Cary, what's that supposed to mean?"

"Just this," Cary said, "and I really do mean it. I hope you'll never lie to keep *me* from worrying."

He put down the phone without saying good-bye.

"Why can't anyone see things the way I do?" Jane complained to Andy. "I mean, you and Toby and Cary act like I'm some kind of a criminal or something. All I'm trying to do is spare my parents' feelings."

"Or is it *your* feelings?" asked Andy. "I'm not sure if you are sorrier about losing the pearls or suffering an 'I-told-you-so' from your mother."

"Andy, you must be joking. You know how much I loved that necklace. It's just that I know I'll get it back. And in the meantime, I don't want to upset everyone."

Jane was up and dressed now, trying haphazardly to tidy up her side of the room, in case her mother and father stopped by after lunch. As she put each shirt and sweater and jacket in drawers and on hangers, she checked pockets for the pearls. She even shook her shoes before putting them in the seldom-used shoe bag that hung on the closet door.

"What makes you so sure the pearls will turn up?" Andy asked.

"Because I wished very hard. On my birthday. It was special. Like Toby said, I was sixteen on the sixteenth of September. And don't you remember — all the other wishes came true, just like magic?"

"That's true." Andy, still in her striped pajamas did a couple of stretches, her bare foot against the wall. "Well, they may turn up." Her voice sounded doubtful. "If we don't find them by tomorrow, we can call the police."

"The police?" Jane's eyes grew big.

"Sure." Andy stretched the other leg. "If the pearls are insured, you'll have to have a police report in order to file a claim. I remember that — from when my mother lost her wedding ring in the salad greens."

"We could check on Henry," said Jane, her face brightening with hope. "See if he has a record. Except we don't have his last name."

"His initials were on the strap of his creel. HCS. And, don't forget, I snapped his picture."

"So you see," said Jane. "There's every reason to think we'll get them back."

'Uh-huh," said Andy with a shrug. She went to her dresser drawer and pulled out a fresh blue leotard.

"I see you're not going to take me up on the lunch invitation," said Jane, looking a little hurt. Toby had raced off with Neal, saying after some hesitation that they probably wouldn't be back in time for lunch. But maybe she could see Jane's parents later that afternoon. Now Andy was bowing out, too.

"Uh, I need to practice today," said Andy.

"Lunch won't take that long," said Jane. "I think I'm going to need some moral support."

"You know, Jane," said Andy, "you have my support no matter what. But I just can't sit there and wait for the bomb to drop. Waiting for your mother to say 'Why didn't you wear the necklace, dear?' Sorry, but my stomach just isn't up to all that suspense."

"I suppose you think mine *is*," said Jane.

"But you don't have to do this to yourself," said Andy. "If you faced your mother and got it over with, you could stop worrying."

"You make it sound so simple," said Jane, slamming shut her dresser drawer. "But you don't know my family. They're just not understanding, like yours."

"You might be right," said Andy. "My family is always very understanding." She slipped on the leotard and her peach-colored warm-up socks and tied her running shoes. "But there's one thing they don't understand. And neither do I."

"And that is?"

Andy left her words behind her as she headed out the door. "Why anyone would lie to people they love."

Jane slumped back on her bed. Now she felt more than anxious. She felt angry. And very much alone. Sure, people were always around for the fun. But now that she was in trouble, her two dearest friends had walked out on her. Make that *three* dearest friends. Cary had practically hung up on her. Whatever answer she could find for her problem, she'd have to find it on her own.

An off-key voice was singing in the hall. "Happee Burthday to youuu. . . ." Seconds later Dee popped in from next door, carrying a string of sagging balloons, pale lavender ones that matched the wide stripes in her T-shirt. "Some big party last night!" she said. "If you think these balloons are deflated, you should have seen your birthday guests!"

"Oh, I'm really sorry," said Jane. "We had some trouble getting back."

"Merry told us at breakfast," Dee said cheerfully. "You're forgiven. Belated Happy Birthday, anyway."

"Thanks. Thanks a lot."

"If you were partying up a storm," said Dee in her best Laguna Beach Californiese, "how come you got becalmed? Hey, get it, that's a pun."

"Ho-ho," said Jane, who couldn't manage a sincere laugh.

"So tell me," said Dee, tossing the balloons in the air. "How was it?"

"The birthday? Oh, it was fine. Just fine!"

"Fine? That's all it was?"

"I mean wonderful. Really."

"You could have fooled me. You look like you've lost your last friend."

"Not quite," said Jane. "But almost." Then she rolled over onto her pillow and broke into tears.

"Hey, come on," said Dee, her tanned face paling. "I'm from the sunshine state, remember? No rain allowed." She sat down on the bed and put her arm around Jane's shoulders. And along with her tears, Jane spilled out her sorrows. Troubles that seemed to have less to do with lost pearls than lost friends.

Dee reached over the top of her dresser to a small hinged box. It had a Japanese woman with a fan on the top. As she touched the lid, a music box began to play "Love is a Many Splendored Thing."

She reached through a tangle of beads. "Here's your answer." In her hand was a string of pearls.

"They're very nice," Jane said. "But I wouldn't dare. I might lose these, too."

"Be my guest," Dee said. "Six dollars at the Orange County swap meet."

Maggie, from her desk, appraised the pearls with a critical eye. "Or you can borrow mine," she said. She got up and opened her chest of drawers. "I think they're fairly good ones. My father brought them from The Orient."

Jane held up both strands and looked in the mirror. "Actually, Dee's look a little more like mine," she said. "Because the pearls are graduated. Except the ones in the middle are a little smaller."

Jane put the strand around her neck, clasped it and looked in the mirror again. "They look fine," said Maggie. "But not exactly like your great-grandmother's." In her excitement Friday evening, Jane had shown her treasure not only to Maggie and Dee, but to everyone on the fourth floor.

"It's okay," said Dee. "Jane can wear a blouse with a high neckline. Or button up her blouse." She turned to Jane. "What outfit did you have in mind?"

"For lunch today, just an oxford shirt and jeans," said Jane. "Which will be fine. The necklace will fall below the shirt opening. Like it does with this one." With the trauma of this teary morning, Jane was still in her tailored Ralph Lauren button-down nightshirt.

"And what about at dinner this evening?"

Jane frowned. "That's another story. I've looked through my entire closet. All the necklines of my dresses are rounded or scooped. Except for the heavy winter things that have cowls or turtlenecks."

"Maybe we can lend you something," said Maggie.

"Thanks, but that's okay. If I can get through lunch, I'll be fine. Tonight I'll just dash out in a hurry and pretend I forgot them. Or — maybe even better — I'll say that Meredith went out and I couldn't get into the safe. Once my mother and father have seen the pearls at lunch, they won't be suspicious, right?"

"Right," said Maggie.

Dee shook her head. It was hard for Jane to tell if the nod meant dismay or admiration. "You always said you wanted to be a writer," Dee said. "And I must say, you sure are getting good at fiction!"

CHAPTER TWELVE

Toby clomped into the room later Sunday afternoon, drew off her boots, put her hat on the dresser, next to the frame that held the pictures of her father and of her horse, Max. She put the tennis racket she carried under the bed and tossed her rolled-up tennis togs into the corner. Her manner was bouncy, her face rosy. "It's been quite a weekend!" she crowed to Jane and Andy "Yesterday sailing and swimming. Today three sets of tennis and a ten-mile ride. I feel like an NBC Sunday Sportscast." She picked up her towel, her soap, and toothbrush. "How did it go for you, Jane? I mean, uh, with your parents."

"Beautifully," said Jane. "We had a lovely lunch. That is, if you call Greaf-burgers lovely."

"No joke, you went to the diner?" Toby couldn't quite picture the elegant Gloria Barrett in a high-backed booth, reading a typed menu encased in greasy plastic.

"Cary was a doll," said Jane. "He really went all out to make the big impression. Served the burgers open-faced on a steak platter with Dijon mustard sauce, radish roses, and carrot curleycues. Then he unplugged the jukebox and played Rachmaninoff's Concerto Number 3 on his portable stereo as background music. He came up with a fancy routine, bowing and saying 'My name is Cary. I'll be your waitperson.' They thought he was adorable."

"Whew," Toby said. "I'm glad it went well. But what about — "

"The pearls?" Andy completed the question. "That went fine, too."

"Look!" said Jane. She pulled a strand from under her pink button-down shirt.

"You found them; Oh, Jane, that's the best news since Texas got statehood."

"Well, not exactly. Look closer." Toby looked closer, her face blank. Pearls were pearls.

"They're Dee's," said Andy. "She lent them to Jane. And her mother didn't even notice."

"Oh, she noticed all right. She said right off, 'I see you saved your pearls for a special occasion.' And I said, 'Lunch with my family is a very special occasion!' And my mother said, 'Well, I must say, this is a day to remember.' My father didn't say anything, he was thinking about a side of onion rings."

"Well, that's a relief," Toby said. "It doesn't exactly solve your problem, but at least it postpones it for a while."

Jane kicked off her loafers and drew her feet up on the bed. With her legs straight out in front of her, she waggled her toes in their pink socks. "Tonight I'm going to pretend that I put the pearls in Meredith's safe. Then I'll say she went out. So after my parents leave, I'll have plenty of time to find them."

"But what if you don't?" said Andy.

Jane heaved an impatient sigh. "Don't be silly. Of course I'll find them. I told you, I wished it on my birthday. And, as you said Toby, all wishes on a special birthday like mine are bound to come true."

"I said, *maybe* they'll come true. But if I were you, Jane, I wouldn't stake my future on a birthday wish. At least not one that wasn't in my control."

"Thanks a lot, friend," said Jane. "I thought you and Andy would stick with me in any kind of trouble. Now you turn against me. You try to ruin any hope I have of getting out of this mess." Her eyes grew bright with unspilled tears.

"We're not against you, Jane," Toby said. "We just think a little honesty would come in handy right now."

"If you ask me," Andy said, "I think Jane

can't be honest with her parents because she's not honest with herself. She still can't admit that the pearls are lost."

"They're not lost!" Jane insisted, pounding her fists on the quilt. "I just can't find them!"

"See what I mean?" said Andy.

"Jane," said Toby, "if wishes count for anything, you know that Andy and I want more than anything for you to find the pearls. We'll wish on the evening star, we'll blow the fuzz off a dandelion, we'll give you all our wishbones from the cafeteria chicken."

"We'll search for four-leaf clovers in the Baker lawn," said Andy brightly.

"But we still think you ought to tell your parents," Toby said, picking up her towel.

The phone bleated. Andy picked it up. "Oh, hello, Mrs. Barrett. This is Andy. How are you? Yes, she's here." She handed the receiver to Jane.

"When are you coming by?" Jane asked. "You're here? Now? I thought our reservation was at six. Uh, sure. That's fine. Just fine!"

Jane's hand shook as she put down the phone. "My mother's downstairs and on her way up. I wonder why she's so early." She tore off Dee's necklace and dropped it in the top dresser drawer."

"I'd better get in the shower," said Toby, heading for the door. "Neal's taking me for pizza at five-thirty before he heads home."

"I, er, have to get to the library," said Andy.

"The library's closed on Sunday afternoon," said Jane.

"Then I've got to borrow a book from Maggie," Andy answered.

"I can't believe you wouldn't want to say hello to my mother. What's the matter with you two?"

"Of course. We should say hi to Mrs. Barrett, Toby. And thank her for the party."

"Sure," said Toby. "But then I have to rush."

"Me, too," said Andy.

"Please, you two, don't leave me!" Jane pleaded in a whisper.

At that moment Gloria Barrett walked in. She was dressed casually, like a school girl, in a striped cotton shirt, full corduroy skirt and penny loafers. But she wore them with gold bangle bracelets and a very voguish air. All three girls rose to their feet as they had been taught to do. "Hello, Mrs. Barrett," Toby and Andy chimed.

"I'm happy to see you," said Mrs. Barrett. Her tone was friendly, but she was not smiling.

"We had a wonderful time on Jane's birthday," said Andy.

"We really did,' 'said Toby.

"I'm glad you enjoyed the day," said Gloria Barrett. She still had not flickered a smile.

"Where's Father?" said Jane. She pulled

out her desk chair for her mother, but Mrs. Barrett did not sit down.

"He's resting back at the Inn. I wanted to see you alone for a few minutes, so I slipped out when he turned on the football game."

"We have to go, anyway," said Andy.

"No, I'd like you girls to stay a minute," said Jane's mother, "if you don't mind."

Jane felt a small shiver down her spine. Her friends — if they were friends — had better not leave her.

"I'll get right to the point, Jane," said Mrs. Barrett. "Where are the pearls?"

"Uh, they're in Meredith's safe," Jane lied.

"Would you go get them, please?"

"Meredith's not home this afternoon," said Jane, thankful she'd prepared this excuse in advance.

"I suppose she wasn't home this morning, either," Gloria Barrett said. "Otherwise you would have worn the pearls to lunch."

"But I did . . ." said Jane. She paused in mid-sentence, realizing she was trapped.

"That's right," said Andy. "Merry's been gone all day."

"I'm afraid you're mistaken, Andy," said Mrs. Barrett, "I just saw her downstairs, coming from the kitchen. She said you were going to have another party tonight, a post-birthday for the girls on your floor."

"That's right," Andy said, and she began

jabbering a mile a minute. "The girls have blown up balloons and we're having the left-over cake and ice cream and tons of sodas and chips and popcorn. . . ."

"And chutney and oysters," said Toby.

A silence followed. Then Mrs. Barrett said again, in a low but impatient voice. "Jane. *Where* are the pearls?"

"Don't worry, Mother. They're safe."

"They're out being washed. I mean cleaned!" blurted Toby.

"They're being restrung," said Andy. "The thread broke. But it was knotted," she added, "so we didn't lose any."

Mrs. Barrett shook her head sadly. Her answer was soft, her words slow and distinct. "Great-grandmother's pearls," she said, "were strung on a gold chain."

CHAPTER THIRTEEN

Jane and her mother ambled slowly across the campus of Canby Hall, over the cement walks through the lawns lined with gigantic trees, from Baker to Addison to Charles. They walked with their heads down, as if their loafers — which were identical dark brown Bass Weejuns — were something important to watch.

"I can't believe you'd do that to me, Jane."

Jane brushed away a tear with the back of her wrist. "But, Mother, it's not as if I lost the pearls on purpose. I mean, I was really very careful. Up to a point."

Her mother sighed, a sigh that was sadder than tears. "You still don't understand, do you?"

"How much you valued the necklace? Of course I do. I mean it wasn't just that it was expensive. There was a lot of sentiment at-

tached. That's why I couldn't bear to tell you
I lost it."

Gloria Barrett and her daughter passed the
tennis courts and the skating pond, where a
mother duck was leading a chain of six duck-
lings on a quiet swim through the dark water.
Jane wondered if they would be old enough to
fly south by the time the pond froze.

"Jane, let me tell you a story. When I was
about your age, a little younger — fifteen I
think — my parents gave me a lovely gold
wristwatch. It was trimmed with diamonds
and had tiny rubies instead of numerals.
Mother had cautioned me to keep it in its special black satin box, and wear it only on
Sundays or special days. But I loved that
watch so much, I took it to bed with me every
night. It was the first thing I looked at in the
morning, and the last before going to sleep."

Her mother cleared her throat, walked a
few steps, her footsteps crunching a few syca-
more leaves, before she continued. "One
morning I awoke and found the watch lying
on the floor. My cat, Snowball, had knocked it
from the table beside my bed onto the tiles
of the hearth. The crystal that protects the
face was shattered. In my shock I panicked.
I knew my parents would be furious that I
had been so careless with their expensive gift
— even though, believe it or not, I still blame
Snowball. I thought the watch was damaged
beyond repair. So, do you know what I did?

Rather than have my mother discover the broken watch, I buried it."

"Oh, Mother, you didn't!" A faint smile crossed Jane's lips.

"But I did!" Now Mrs. Barrett not only smiled, she stifled a small giggle. "Imagine!

"The point of the story is this," she went on. "If I had been honest with my mother, I would have saved myself months of pain — the guilt and worry I suffered while I waited for my parents to discover the loss. When I finally confessed what I had done — the following spring after the snows had melted — we uncovered the watch where I had hid it, under the deodar tree. Of course, by that time it was beyond repair. I wrapped the rusty mess in a piece of tissue paper, tied it with a blue ribbon, and returned it to the satin box. And I kept that black box next to my bed to remind me never to lie again."

Jane walked a few steps in silence. "Oh, Mother, that is such a sad story."

"Yes, it is, Jane. But the sad part is not the loss of the watch, but how my lack of honesty — and lack of courage — caused both me and my parents to suffer needlessly."

"That's right," said Jane.

"You remember the old saying, 'A coward dies a thousand deaths, the brave man but one?' You will find as the years go by that you will suffer more from lack of courage than any other pain."

"I suppose you're right," said Jane, not sounding convinced.

"Tell me," said Gloria Barrett, "don't you feel much better, now that I know about the pearls?"

"Well, of course. But that's because you've been so great. I mean you are being super-understanding."

"Have I ever given you any reason to think I might not understand your problems?"

"Well, uh, no. Except, I wasn't sure you'd understand about Cary and me."

"But when you brought him home and faced your father and me with what you thought might be a problem — suddenly it disappeared, didn't it?"

"Well, yes, I guess it did."

"Granted, your father and I did have our doubts about Cary. But now we are quite fond of him. At lunch today he was a dear."

By this time Jane and her mother had reached the wishing pond. They sat on a stone bench beside it. "Young people never realize how much it hurts parents when, no matter how kind and sympathetic they try to be, are always told 'You don't understand.' You'd be surprised how much we do understand. I've told you my little tale of woe — which embarrasses me to this day — to let you know that once upon a time, and not as many years ago as it might seem, I was a girl exactly your age." She gave a slight laugh. "After all, contrary to common opinion, we parents weren't born adults."

Jane sighed. "I wish I could be an adult right now, and not have to go on making silly mistakes."

"You're at the wishing pond." Mrs. Barrett reached into her purse and handed Jane a dime.

"No. No more wishes," said Jane. "They're what got me into trouble in the first place. Wishing my problem would solve itself. Instead of facing up to it like I should have."

Mrs. Barrett cast the ten-cent piece into the water and watched the wide circles spread to the edge of the pond.

"Did *you* wish?" asked Jane.

"No," said her mother. "I think I owed for yours. Your words just now — about facing up — sounded incredibly adult!"

Gloria Barrett put her arm around Jane's shoulders as they walked back to Baker. "The pearls were precious," she said, "because they were a symbol of the love that the Barretts have for one another. Now they're gone, but our love remains the same. Remember that, and we'll have no more such trouble."

"Oh, I will, Mother. At least I'll try to." She put her arm around her mother's slender waist. "Thanks a lot. I mean, you are such a wonderful mom!" Arm-in-arm they walked, their steps lighter and quicker, back toward Baker.

"And now you'd best hurry, dear. Your father will be waiting."

Jane stopped and faced her mother. "Does he know? About the pearls?"

"Not now. But I'm sure he will by dinnertime." She drew back and looked Jane straight in the eye. "Won't he?"

Jane gave her mother a peck on the cheek. "Yes, of course he will!"

The candlelight flickered against his glass as David French Barrett raised a toast to his daughter. "Happy birthday, sweet sixteen!"

Jane looked across at her father and mother, then lowered her eyes toward the base of the silver candelabra. "Not so sweet, maybe, but happy. It was my best birthday ever."

"That's what growing older is all about," said Jane's father. "Granted, every year is going to have its bumpy spots." He smiled and shook his head. "Like you had this weekend. . . ."

Jane's father paused and looked at her across the table. Jane put her hand to her throat and felt an emptiness where her beautiful pearls should be.

"But if you face your problems — like you did tonight — and learn from them, there's no reason that each birthday can't be happier than all the ones that went before."

"If only that were true," Jane said, her eyes bright. "I'd have a lot to look forward to."

"You do," said her mother.

"Yes, you do," said David Barrett as he nodded to his wife and covered her hand with his.

CHAPTER FOURTEEN

Jane hugged her mother and father as they stood on the front porch of Baker. "Thank you again. For the happiest birthday ever. And for being the nicest parents in the world." She opened the heavy oak door and turned to watch them as they went down the steps. The Baker entry hall was lit, the social room, too, but no one was around.

She climbed the stairs to the fourth floor, not really wanting this Sunday to end. Jane felt a little dreamy as she thought back over the past few hours. How much had changed since she talked to her mother. It was as if a year had passed instead of a day. She felt older. And much wiser. If this was what it meant to grow up, she was all for it.

Anxious to share her feelings with her two best friends, she hurried down the hall to Room 407. The floor was strangely quiet, no radios blasting, no wild whoops of laughter.

And 407 was dark. She flicked the wall switch, which turned on the milk-glass lamp by her bed. How disappointing to come home to an empty room. She went next door to Dee and Maggie's room. A small desk light was on, but there were no signs of life. The bedspreads were not even crumpled.

Back in 407 Jane went to the desk for her notebook. She wanted to put down some of her thoughts about the birthday weekend. The importance of this day went way beyond its fantastic celebration. Or her fabulous gift — a gift that had disappeared so quickly it seemed to have existed only in a dream.

Jane turned on her stereo and tuned it to the public radio station. Now that she was an adult, she would have to turn her mind to adult issues — things like apartheid and world hunger.

On her desk was a note from Merry "Please check in with me as soon as you get in. Important."

Jane's heart leapt. Perhaps, just perhaps, Merry had some news about the pearls. Her heart continued pounding as she dashed up the stairs to Merry's apartment. But no, she kept warning herself. No more false hopes. Face the truth. Still, her hand shook a little as she knocked on Merry's door.

Merry had a strange look on her face as she opened the door. "Oh, yes, Jane. Come in."

"Surprise!" shouted a roomful of faces,

with Toby and Andy in front. "Happy un-birthday to you!" they sang. All of the fourth floor was packed into Meredith's small apartment, their heads bobbing in and out of dozens of freshly inflated balloons and pink and purple crepe paper streamers. Over the streamers were gobs of confetti strings, as if a a wild New Year's Eve party were in full swing. Jane made her way through the paper jungle. "Honestly," she giggled. "This is too crazy! A planned surprise un-birthday party. And the funny part of it — this *is* a surprise. I'd forgotten our plans for tonight. At least, temporarily."

"We figured you might," said Dee. "But since you slipped up yesterday, we weren't going to let you get away with it again. And if you didn't show — we were ready to go ahead anyway."

Maggie turned on Meredith's stereo, playing Cary's tape of "Come on Out, Jane" full blast.

"We're hungry," said Andy. "Come blow out your cake candles and let's get going." She put a match to sixteen fresh candles on the slightly-eaten sheet cake. One extra candle stood on the other end. "And since you're now sixteen-plus, here's one to grow on."

"Make a wish," said Dee.

Jane hesitated in front of the blaze of candles. "Oh, dear, not that again," she said to herself. But after thinking a moment she said aloud, "I wish that all my birthdays will be this happy." Then she blew out all the candles in one huff, all but the seventeenth at the other end, which flickered and smoked, then relit itself.

"Oh, well," said Jane, with a shrug.

"It doesn't matter, anyway," said Toby. "That one was extra."

"No, it doesn't matter," said Jane. "I don't believe in wishes any more. Only hopes and dreams."

"Wishes, hopes, dreams, what's the difference?" Dee asked.

"Wishes are for things beyond our power," Jane said matter-of-factly. "But we can work for our hopes and dreams." She began slicing the cake into squares and putting it on small paper plates. Andy went to Meredith's freezer for the ice cream.

"Wait," Jane said. "First we should finish off the rest of the feast. Ice cream and cake for dessert."

"And only if you eat your vegetables," Andy cracked. She closed the freezer and the party guests dutifully lined up with larger paper plates — pink and purple ones with confetti designs — heaping them with handfuls of chips and spoonfuls of dip, raw vegetables, melon slices, candied popcorn, marshmallows. Cold cuts, cheese, peanut butter, raisins. Then Jane's brie, pate, and smoked oysters.

Maggie took a smoked oyster and looked at

it suspiciously. "Is it really true that sometimes people find pearls in these things?"

Toby blushed and looked over toward her roommate. She knew that Jane would be reminded of her loss. At this point Toby wished that oysters had never invented pearls.

But Jane seemed oblivious of her friend's thoughtless remark. "I had such a lovely dinner with my parents," she said. "Rack of lamb with mint sauce. I can't believe an hour later everything tastes so good!"

Andy caught Jane's meaning. It had nothing to do with roast lamb. Their eyes met. "So everything is fine with your folks?"

"Couldn't be better," said Jane.

Toby looked at Jane in wonder. She was sure it *could* be better — if Jane were able to find her pearls. Or was that the way it went with rich people? As they say, "Easy come, easy go."

Meredith tapped a spoon on her glass of Diet Coke. "While we were waiting, we played a little game," she said. "We passed around a slip of paper and had everyone compose an instant two-line verse about our guest of honor. We only allowed each writer sixty seconds, so don't expect any Shakespeare. But from what I see here, we may have a few budding poets in the group. They will, of course, remain anonymous."

The party guests sipped on their sodas as

Meredith, trying to keep a straight face, read the birthday verses.

> We all thought Bostonians were straight
>   as a stick.
> But you are quite the mellow chick.

Mellow chick. That sounded like Dee talk, thought Jane.

> A girl has to have a lot of pizazz,
> To capture Cary, the king of rock jazz.
> She's blonde, blue-eyed and wears big
>   smiles.
> Her *floor* wears the latest preppy styles.

The group cracked up at this one. Jane looked from face to face to uncover the author. No one gave herself away.

> Someday, Jane, you'll write a novel.
> Will you be famous or live in a hovel?

> Jane Barrett comes from old Boston.
> She's just *boss* and a *ton* of fun.

Jane, her face coloring, watched the grinning faces as Merry read the very personal, teasing, and badly metered tributes. She was deeply touched.

"And last, I'll read you my own contribution," Meredith said, "which makes me wonder why I thought up this game in the first place!"

Jane you're as sweet as cake and ice
    cream.
I hope you capture your birthday dream.

The girls laughed and applauded Meredith's effort.

"Speaking of which," Andy said, "let's get to the dessert!"

She and Toby brought out the ice cream cartons and put a taste of the three flavors on each girl's plate next to the cake square, then set out the three kinds of toppings.

When they were all seated, mostly cross-legged on the floor, Andy announced, "The cake has fortune surprises in it, wrapped in foil. So be careful. Don't chomp down too hard."

"Hey, I was wondering who was trying to knock out my molars." Dee said, holding up a tiny package. She unwrapped it and held up the toy diamond ring.

"You'll be the first to be engaged," said Andy. Everyone cheered.

"Now, all I need is a big, blond surfer," said Dee, slipping on the ring and admiring her tanned left hand. Jane looked on smiling. How far away yesterday seemed, when she would actually have cheated to get that dime-store ring.

"I got a key!" Toby said. "What does that mean?"

"Success and fame," said Andy, with a slight shadow of disappointment on her face.

"Oh, I'm not worried about that," said Toby. "Give me an acre of ground and a pair of horses, and I'll be just fine. She handed the key over to Andy. "Here," she said. "For your brilliant ballet career!"

Jane meanwhile had found the wrapped dime in her square. She felt a pang of disappointment that someone more deserving — like either of her roommates — had not received it. But it would seem odd to give it away, as if to say she already had enough money. She put the coin down quietly on Meredith's coffee table.

"Who got the dime?" Andy asked.

When no one answered Jane said rather shame-facedly, "I did."

Andy laughed. "The dime stands for wealth," she explained to others. "You see, these fortunes really do work!"

"And what is this for?" Maggie asked. "Wisdom?" She held up a cake-covered string of beads. "Pearls of wisdom?"

"Hey, wait!" said Andy, puzzled.

Jane blanched and rushed across the room to Maggie. "Pearls!"

She took the chocolately strand from Maggie, raced to Merry's sink and rinsed it. Then she burst into tears. "My pearls, I've found my pearls!"

CHAPTER FIFTEEN

Clutching the pearls tightly in her hand, Jane dashed back to 407. After putting the necklace carefully in its blue velvet box, she put the box on the nightstand next to her bed. Then she raced to the phone at the end of the hall and dialed the Greenleaf Inn. Her mother's sleepy voice answered the phone.

"Jane, dear, are you all right?" Any phone call after ten p.m. spelled trouble to Mrs. Barrett.

"I'm not just all right. I'm perfect!" said Jane, practically shouting. "Guess what? I found the pearls!"

"Oh, Oh! Darling. how wonderful. Where on earth were they? Did you hear that, David? Jane has found the pearls!"

David French Barrett, dead asleep, rolled over in his paisley pajamas. "Mmph, hrumph. Girls? What girls?"

"The pearls. Your grandmother's pearls."

At this he sat up straight in bed, rubbed his eyes and said, "I must be dreaming. You said you found the pearls."

"Jane, tell me, where were they?"

Jane gave an embarrassed giggle. "Well, you're not going to believe me. They were in my birthday cake."

"Your birthday cake. Oh, dearest, why did you put them *there?*"

"I didn't really *put* them there, Mother. They just went there all by themselves."

Mrs. Barrett sighed into the telephone. "I guess I'm getting old or something. Or are you not making sense?"

Jane's laugh was breathless in her excitement. "You see, I was putting the cake in the oven and the boat came about and Cary fell overboard and the pearls fell into the cake batter. I didn't notice because my face went into the batter, too."

"It's late. I'm just not getting all this," said Mrs. Barrett. "But you're telling me the pearls are safe and that you're fine."

"I'm perfect," Jane said.

"I've always thought that, dear," her mother said.

"Hi, Cary. Guess what? I found them, I found them!"

Cary stared at the shouting telephone receiver, as if it were lying to him. "The pearls?" he said. "Wow!" He shot a jubilant whistle into the phone, "Tell me. What stone did we leave unturned?"

"They were in the cake. Maggie Morrison almost ate them!"

"In the cake? You're kidding."

Jane went on about finding the chocolate-coated necklace.

Cary's answers were brief. "Yeah? No way. Great." He sounded a little distracted.

"What's the matter?" asked Jane. "I thought you'd be bouncing up and down like I am.

"Hey, don't get me wrong," Cary said. "I'm really happy for you, Jane. But on this end I've had a little bad news."

"What's the matter?" Jane asked, for the moment forgetting her joy. Cary sounded really down. And that wasn't like him.

"I'm grounded next weekend," he said.

"Oh, come on. Because you were late last night? But we had an excuse. We didn't even get to shore until almost midnight. Have the dorm counselor call Meredith. Or even the Coast Guard."

"That's the problem. Ames, our regular counselor, is taking his LSAT this week. So meanwhile we've got this substitute turkey, who's trying to make the big impression for discipline. Bill Pickett. We call him Picky Bill."

"A real stickler, you mean."

"You got it," said Cary. "The minute he hears the word *but*, he turns and walks away."

"Oh, Cary, I'm sorry."

"So that's it for the Hillsboro Homecoming."

"Oh, Cary!" All her excitement about the necklace faded.

For some reason Jane felt as if Cary's problem were all her fault. If she just hadn't happened to have a birthday. No sooner does one hurdle get jumped than another pops up to take its place.

"Two-hundred bucks they were paying us. A big two hundred dollars out the window. That was going into our recording fund." He paused and cleared his throat. "I didn't tell you. It was going to be a surprise. When we got enough money together, we were going to cut a single. Send it out to disc jockeys. Now that's all dust. If we don't show up for Hillsboro, who's going to hire us? By the time we get the cash together, our rock group will be in rockers."

"There's got to be something you can say or do," Jane said. "That just isn't right."

"You're telling me! The guys have been practicing every day this week for their big break. And now *they're* being punished because of me."

"And you're being punished because of me," said Jane. The search for the pearls had delayed their trip home until after the wind had died down. If she hadn't been given the pearls. If she'd been more careful with the pearls. If she hadn't been spoiled with that birthday party in the first place. If, if, if. "It's all my fault," she said. "My birthday got us into all kinds of trouble. Sometimes I wish my parents weren't so —" She stopped. No more wishes, Jane, remember? "It isn't fair," she said. "It just isn't fair."

"Where'd you get the crazy idea," he replied, "that life is fair?"

CHAPTER SIXTEEN

Halfway home from Spanish class Toby began hoping for a letter. It was crazy to hope for one so soon, but that was the last thing Neal had said, his lips against her cheek, "I'll write."

That could mean a week or two or even a month! So four days was a little soon to start thinking about a letter in the mail slot marked Houston. But Toby couldn't help herself. A thick letter on creme-colored stationery embossed with Cornelius Worthington III, inscribed in Neal's strong handwriting. The thought of it made Toby tingle with excitement. But when she walked into Baker, the 407 letterbox was empty.

She met Jane on the stairs, on her way down to lunch. Jane had several envelopes in her hand. "Andy's already in the dining room. Don't bother to go upstairs. I have our mail." She put the letters behind her back. "Some very important mail, as it turns out."

"Anything for me?" Toby asked, trying to act casual.

"Could be," Jane teased.

Toby's heart gave a hopeful thump. "Who from?"

"I'll give you three guesses," Jane said, with a sneaky smile.

"No fair, Jane, don't tease me."

"Tease you? I wouldn't think of it." With that she waved a creme-colored envelope at Toby and raced into the dining room.

"Come on, hand it over," Toby pleaded as she approached Jane, seated next to Andy at one of the small wooden tables. Jane was fanning herself with the letter. "Andy, make her behave."

"Shape up, Jane," Andy said, "or you'll have no one to share your lonely Saturday night with."

The thought sobered Jane, and she handed Toby Neal's letter.

"Thanks," she said, her green eyes bright with anticipation. "Why don't I hold the table while you two get your trays." Toby was hoping for a few moments alone with Neal's letter.

"No, that's okay," said Andy. "It's not as if we're dying to load up on Baked Loch Ness Monster with gill sauce."

Laughing, Jane put her hand to her mouth as if she were suddenly ill. "Or steamed potatoes with thousand staring eyes."

Andy and Jane sat silently as Toby opened the letter. They saw her look of disappointment, at the single sheet of note paper. A check fell out of the fold. It was signed by Neal and made out to Jane.

"Here's a check for you, Jane," Toby said, with a puzzled look.

"For me?" Jane asked. "How strange."

Dear Toby,

Just a note to thank you for a wonderful weekend. There is no place I'd rather be than sailing. And no one I'd rather be sailing with than you. Thanks so much for inviting me. And thank Jane for her birthday hospitality.

My friend Roger insists the battery problem was his fault and is refunding the rental fee. He hopes it didn't spoil our day. How's that for a nice guy?

So now maybe you three can plan another feast. No, ouch. My stomach still hurts!

Please turn this check over to Jane. If she wants another day of sailing, count me in. And if she doesn't, you and I will try another day on the water. What's say, sailor?

I'll write a *real* letter as soon as I have cooled my Biology exam.

Meanwhile, I'm thinking of you, Green Eyes.

Much love,
Neal.

* * *

Toby put the letter to her face. It was short but it said all the things she had wanted to hear. She smiled and stashed it quickly in her shirt pocket. Tonight before bed she would read it a dozen more times.

"Good letter, huh?" said Andy.

"Good letter," said Toby with a small sigh.

"But what about the check?" asked Jane.

"Oh, the check. Yes. Roger's refunding your money. Because the battery was dead."

"How nice!" Jane looked the check over. "That's incredibly nice, as a matter of fact."

"Whoopee! Now what happens?" asked Andy "Another birthday?"

Jane thought of all the problems her birthday celebration had caused — especially the latest one for Cary.

"I think our celebrations are over for a while," she sighed.

"You can buy yourself a super-dooper gift," Toby suggested.

Jane got up from the table and headed for the lunch line. "Now that I have my pearls back, I can't think of a thing I'd want."

Not quite true. By the time she had put the carrot-raisin salad on her tray, Jane knew just the gift she would buy herself — something she wanted in the worst way.

CHAPTER SEVENTEEN

"Come on downtown with me," Jane said to her roommates after school on Friday afternoon. She wore a mysterious smile. "I'm going to cash Neal's check and get my belated birthday present."

"So you thought of something you need?" asked Toby. For the life of her, she couldn't imagine anything Jane Barrett would be lacking.

"Something I need a lot," said Jane, with a sly smile. "But I may also need some help getting it home."

"Is it alive?" asked Andy.

"In a way," Jane said. "At least part of it." She was in one of her maddening tease moods again. "And it might be heavy. So if you come along, I'll treat for ice cream. Or pizza." Jane knew her roommates would come along just for friendship's sake. But a small bribe made it more fun. "We'd better hurry, the bank closes at four o'clock."

"Then you can use the cash machine."

Jane shook her blonde curls. "Not today," she said.

"I just hope," said Andy, "that whatever it is — you're going to keep it outside 407. This place is beginning to look like a garage sale."

"And we certainly don't want any large partly-alive animal in here," said Toby.

When they reached the bank Jane stood on the little flowered rug that said "Wait here," until a cashier became available. Then she deposited Neal's check and made out a withdrawal slip for one hundred and seventy-five dollars. "I'd like that all in ones," she said.

The cashier, a plumpish lady with strawberry hair, looked over her rimless glasses. "In ones?"

"If it's not too much trouble," said Jane.

"Not at all," said the clerk. She brought out one hundred new ones in a wrapper, then counted out another seventy-five and handed Jane the money in a large envelope. Jane put it in her large satchel-shaped brown bag.

"What are you up to?" asked Andy, who had heard Jane's request for ones.

"You'll see," said Jane, continuing her frustrating mysterious act. "Next stop, the Greenleaf Nursery."

Toby rolled her green eyes with exasperation. "Jane, please tell us. What are you doing?" She'd visited a lot of nurseries in her day, but never one that required cash in one dollar bills.

On Saturday night Cary was in his room reading *Rolling Stone*, an article about Springsteen's fifty-six million dollar income earned singing about working class hardships. Fifty-six million. But one day long ago Springsteen was an unknown, struggling like Cary to get his first break. Would that break ever come to Ambulance? Hillsboro had been polite when he called to cancel their Homecoming booking, but the dance committee chairman had sounded pretty frosted. And with good reason. In desperation, they would have to call The Greeks (nicknamed the Geeks by all who knew their music), the most nowhere band in the state.

Being grounded Saturday evening, Cary was not allowed to accept calls. He had telephoned Jane on his break from the Greaf, but she wasn't in her room at Baker. He needed desperately to talk to her. She had such a wonderful way of snapping him out of his blue funks.

Through the window of the dorm came a familiar sound. Ambulance. Was the group downstairs practicing without him? No, there was his guitar, and his own voice. It was the tape of "Jane, Jane." But with a few voices added. Female voices.

Cary threw open the window and looked down on the lawn. There, singing at the top of their lungs, were girls of 407.

> Hey, Slade, Slade, Slade
> Can you come out and play?
> Can you let down your hair
> Or will you stay up there. . . .

Cary broke into a broad grin. Being grounded he knew he couldn't call down to them, no verbal communication was allowed, especially by Picky Bill, who had stayed in tonight to make sure that Cary fulfilled his punishment. Not that the prefect had any-where to go, anyway. Cary acknowledged the serenade by gesturing wildly, dancing insanely to the music.

At that moment Matt came puffing into the room. He was carrying, in a ten-gallon nursery can, an evergreen tree. "What the. . . ." It was an evergreen tree, and the greenest evergreen Cary had ever seen. Its branches were covered with one-dollar bills.

A small card was attached.

Don't get the idea that money grows on trees. Only once in a while.
                    Love,
                    Jane

Cary was relieved that he couldn't talk to Jane at the moment. He felt much too choked up to speak. Whoever thinks rich girls are stuck up and selfish ought to meet his Jane sometime.

"Well, say something," said Matt.

"This is, this is, well, outrageous!" Cary said breathlessly. "What's it all about? My birthday isn't till spring. And Halloween's a month away."

"Looks more like Christmas, doesn't it?" said Matt. "I could sure dig some of these ornaments on *my* tree." He carried the tree across the room and put it on Cary's desk. A couple of dollar bills floated to the floor. "Jane felt so bad about your missing the Hillsboro Homecoming," said Matt, "especially after Ambulance had practiced so hard for the big break. She felt it was all her fault, losing the pearls and all. She blames herself because you were late getting back."

"It was no one's fault. A dead battery can happen to anyone."

"So when Roger refunded the money —"

"He did? Jane didn't tell me."

"Yeah. Because of the battery. So Jane decided she'd try to make up to Ambulance the money they lost by not playing tonight."

"Radical!" said Cary.

"Unreal!" breathed a voice behind them. It was Picky Bill.

"Uh, we were just settling down to study," said Cary. "It's okay for us to work together, isn't it? I mean since we're both grounded."

"Nope," said Picky Bill. "I'm not allowing you to work together. In fact, I'm not allowing you to work at all."

"But — "

"Why didn't you tell me you had battery trouble?" Picky Bill scratched his head. "And that your band had a playing engagement? I mean, come on, I'm a reasonable guy. I mean, even if you did deserve grounding we could have switched nights. No sense in the whole band being punished."

"But — " said Cary.

"No buts about it," Bill said. "I want you out of here within thirty minutes. And on your way to Hillsboro. With Ambulance. Or would you rather have a few demerits?"

"It's too late," said Cary. "Hillsboro has a band lined up."

Picky Bill took a packet of M&Ms from his shirt pocket, popped a yellow and red one in his mouth, and then offered the package to Matt and Cary. "There's always intermission," he said.

CHAPTER EIGHTEEN

The phone in 407 rang early Sunday morning. Jane, alert and awake for a change, sat down on her freshly made bed to answer it.

"I hope I didn't wake you," came Cary's voice.

"Oh, no," said Jane. "We're dressed and headed for breakfast." She surpressed a small, breathless giggle. "How are you? How did you like your surprise?" Toby and Andy gathered by Jane's bed, anxious to hear Cary's reaction.

"I was blown away," said Cary. "That's one of the nicest things that's ever happened to me."

"It was nothing," said Jane. "Just something I wanted to do."

"You call one hundred and seventy-five dollars nothing? I'm exhausted just counting it."

Jane laughed again. "My father always told me I should learn how to handle money. Believe me, after Toby and Andy and I had paper-clipped one hundred and seventy-five bills onto those sticky branches, we figured we knew!"

Toby and Andy nodded in agreement.

"We got a one hundred and fifty dollar refund on the boat," said Jane.

"Yeah, Matt told me," said Cary. "Neal's friend Roger must be a great guy! But what about the twenty-five dollar bonus?"

"That was the change we had left over from grocery shopping. When Roger returned the money, I honestly couldn't think of anything I wanted to buy with it. Until I thought about helping Ambulance get on the way to fame and fortune."

"Did I ever tell you how great I think you are?"

Blushing slightly, Jane twisted her hair and smiled. "As Andy says, 'The ambulance always comes to the rescue, but how often do you get to rescue the Ambulance?' "

Andy grinned, flattered that Jane had repeated her corny joke. After serenading Cary last night, the girls had returned to their room, "grounding" themselves for the evening in Cary's honor and doing a thorough house-cleaning. Now the place was spotless, the books piled neatly on the desks, pens and notebooks in drawers, awaiting a semester of serious study.

While they were putting together Cary's

surprise, Jane had gone on and on to her skeptical roommates about her new resolution to become an adult: more thoughtful, more careful, more responsible. And willing to face problems as they came. "Sure thing," said Andy. Toby rolled her eyes.

But Jane had immediately demonstrated her good intentions by dumping out her dresser drawers and reorganizing what had, in a very short time, become a shambles.

"Well, if that's the way you're going to play it," said Andy, "we can't let you show us up." After winking at Toby, she straightened her shoes in the closet, refolded her jeans and cleaned out her purse. Taking an old wash cloth, she polished the dusty windowpanes and wiped down the sill.

Toby cleaned her dresser top with tissues, and remade her bed Army-style, bouncing a quarter off the tightly pulled rainbow spread, then settled down to her Spanish book and studied two sections in advance. "Responsibility," she had said, "might even be kind of fun."

"Face it," said Andy. "It's boring."

"But, please, let's keep it up, anyway," pleaded Jane, who knew she'd probably need reinforcement.

This morning, bright-eyed from a good night's sleep, the girls had surveyed the room and reviewed their new intentions with satisfaction. And Toby had decided that, yes, responsibility could be fun, but only after it was over with.

Now on the phone Jane was telling Cary about their self-imposed grounding. "And how did *yours* go?" she asked.

"That's the funny part," said Cary. "There wasn't any. Picky Bill let us out. Or rather sent us out. That's the part I want to tell you about."

"Cary, tell me!" said Jane. "That's unbelievable."

"It would sound better over coffee," said Cary. "Now that I'm flush with cash, let me treat all my tree-trimmers to a jelly donut."

"Apple muffin," said Jane. "Right now?" She looked toward her roommates. "We'd love it. But on the condition you don't spend the dollar bills. They're for the fund — for the future of Ambulance."

"That's the part we have to talk about," said Cary. "Thanks to you, Ambulance's future may be arriving any day."

Matt and Cary, with coffee in front of them, were saving a corner booth at the diner. Cary enjoyed going to The Greaf on his day off so he could be waited on. When Jane slid in next to him, he immediately covered her hand with his. Andy sat on the opposite seat next to Matt, and Toby took the outside. Cary called to the counter boy for two stacks of wheat pancakes and a basket of fresh-baked muffins, which usually came with assorted fruits inside — pineapple, apple, blueberry — depending on the cook's mood or what was left over in the refrigerator.

"So tell me," said Jane, sipping on her ice water, "How did you convince Pickett to let you out?" She paused, wondering for the first time why Cary hadn't called her last night when he was free.

He explained, "It seems that when the tree arrived, Picky Bill followed Matt up to my room, wondering what was going on. I guess he stood outside the door and listened. That's how he heard about the dead battery — how you felt everything was your fault. For losing your pearls. Or for having a birthday in the first place. And that you were sending the money to make up for what the band was losing." Cary reached for his gold earring, and tugged on it slightly. "I guess Bill felt pretty bad that he had caused the whole problem by not listening to our story. So he ordered us out of the dorm — on the condition that we barrel on down to Hillsboro."

"But you told Jane," Andy said, "they already had a band."

"If you use the term loosely," Cary said, raising an eyebrow. He took a swallow of his coffee. "It took me a while to track down the guys; we didn't arrive at Hillsboro until almost ten. By that time the dance needed more than Ambulance. It needed the paramedics!"

"Full-on resuscitation?" asked Andy, who had taken a first-aid course in Chicago.

"When we got there, that dance wasn't a Homecoming," said Matt. "It was a home *going*."

"I told the chairperson," Cary continued, "that since we had let them down on the booking, we'd play the intermission for nothing. Matt helped us set up. We got going just in time to stop the crowd that was lined up for the checkroom."

The waiter brought pancakes to the boys. Jane passed around the basket of muffins, which today were raisin/nut. "So what happened to the Geeks?" she asked. "I mean the Greeks?"

"They hung around for one more set and then bailed. It was too embarrassing, I guess, for them to watch how a few blasts from their synthesizer could clear the floor. Man, it was like a fire drill!"

Cary smiled at last night's recollections. "It was too sad," he mused, picking up his pancake fork. "Even the chaperones wouldn't dance."

"But tell them the best part," said Matt, attacking his stack of cakes, trying to keep the butter and syrup even.

"We played solid from midnight to one-thirty," Cary went on. "The crowd was great; I've never felt like such a hit. And at the end, this girl from Graceport Academy comes up and asks for my card. My card! Shoot, like Ambulance was professional or something. Anyway, they're booking us in December — for their Winter Wonderland."

"Graceport!" said Jane. Everyone in Boston knew Graceport; it was thirty miles from the city and very exclusive.

"So maybe Ambulance will make the circuit, after all," said Cary. He took his still unused knife and fork and did a small drummer routine on the table and the water glasses, ending with a large "Yoweee!"

"Sound's like Ambulance is on its way," said Andy. "With full sirens."

At nine-twenty Sunday night Toby was tucked under her rainbow bedspread. "Goodnight ladies. I'm going to leave you now."

"If we're playing *Name that Tune*, said Andy, it's 'Merrily We Roll Along.' My grandma used to sing us to sleep with that."

"I don't need to be sung to sleep," said Toby.

Jane snickered. "She's ready for a few dreams about you-know-who."

Toby had just finished a chatty telephone conversation with Neal, in which she told him how Jane found the chocolate-covered pearls and how Cary knocked the crowd

dead at the Hillsboro dance. After she put
down the phone Toby had put on pajamas
quickly, a sleepy, contented look on her face.

"It's kind of scary, isn't it," she said from
the corner bed, her red hair across the pillow.
"You know, when everything is going right?
And you wonder how long it can last? Like
this week. It's ended up perfectly." She paused
and put her hands behind her head. "I got an
A on my Spanish test. I beat Gigi in tennis.
Cary turns trouble around." She spread her
arms out, palms up on the bedspread. "And
then, to top it off, tonight Neal calls."

"And — don't forget," Andy added, "I'm a
finalist in the ballet tryouts. Which means I
might finally break out to a solo." She took
off her running shoes, the first step toward
getting to bed. "But I know what you mean,
Toby," she said. "Sometimes you get a little
nervous, wondering how long the good luck
will last — how long it will be until the next
little problem pops us."

"Like taking horses over the hurdles," Toby
said.

"Or jumping the waves at the beach," said
Jane. "You just get over one and — "

"If you don't like it, why do it?" asked
Andy.

"Do what?"

"Jump horses. Or waves," Andy said.

"Hmmm," said Jane. "That's a good question."

The girls were silent for a moment. Toby pulled up the rainbow cover as if to say, no problems allowed here tonight, and rolled over to face the window.

The phone bleated. Jane cringed. Like her mother, she felt any late evening call spelled trouble.

A disturbed voice squawked through the receiver. "Oh, yes, Merry," said Jane.

Toby sat up in her bed. Andy sat down on hers.

"Oh. Oh. I'm sorry, Merry. Oh, how awful!"

Andy and Toby looked at one another as if to say, "Here we go again."

"Why, of course. I'll come right over." Jane put down the phone and slipped on her loafers. "Back in a minute," she said.

Andy jumped to her feet. "What's the matter?" Toby threw back her cover. "What's happened to Merry?"

"She has a small problem," said Jane. "But I can take care of it."

"Not without us," said Andy, reaching for her shoes.

Toby dashed to the closet for her robe. "This is face-the-problems week, remember? And we do it together."

Jane smiled. "Thanks, you two. I knew I could count on you. But, really, this is something I can handle by myself."

"*We'll* be the judge of that," said Toby.

"Come on, Jane," said Andy. "Tell us."

"Well, it seems that Merry's refrigerator has gone on the blink," said a sober-faced Jane. "Which means two quarts of ice cream need to be finished off immediately."

"Well," said Toby, her face sliding into a sly smile. "Whatever we can do to help."

"Hey, all right," said Andy. "Let's go."

The three roommates ran down the hall, Jane in the middle, hugging the shoulders of her friends. "Didn't I just say that?" she giggled. "I knew I could count on you!"

Why has Shelley Hyde, one of the former 407 roommates, come back to Canby Hall? Read The Girls of Canby Hall # 29, A ROOMMATE RETURNS.

The Girls of Canby Hall®

by Emily Chase

School pressures! Boy trouble! Roommate rivalry! The girls of Canby Hall are learning about life and love now that they've left home to live in a private boarding school.

☐ 41212-4	#1	Roommates	$2.50
☐ 40079-7	#2	Our Roommate Is Missing	$2.25
☐ 40080-0	#3	You're No Friend of Mine	$2.25
☐ 41417-8	#4	Keeping Secrets	$2.50
☐ 40082-7	#5	Summer Blues	$2.25
☐ 40083-5	#6	Best Friends Forever	$2.25
☐ 40381-X	#12	Who's the New Girl?	$2.25
☐ 40871-2	#13	Here Come the Boys	$2.25
☐ 40461-X	#14	What's a Girl to Do?	$2.25
☐ 33759-9	#15	To Tell the Truth	$1.95
☐ 33706-8	#16	Three of a Kind	$1.95
☐ 40191-2	#17	Graduation Day	$2.25
☐ 40327-3	#18	Making Friends	$2.25
☐ 41277-9	#19	One Boy Too Many	$2.50
☐ 40392-3	#20	Friends Times Three	$2.25
☐ 40657-4	#21	Party Time!	$2.50
☐ 40711-2	#22	Troublemaker	$2.50
☐ 40833-X	#23	But She's So Cute	$2.50
☐ 41055-5	#24	Princess Who?	$2.50
☐ 41090-3	#25	The Ghost of Canby Hall	$2.50

Complete series available wherever you buy books.

Scholastic Inc.
P.O. Box 7502, 2932 East McCarty Street, Jefferson City, MO 65102

Please send me the books I have checked above. I am enclosing $_____
(please add $1.00 to cover shipping and handling). Send check or money order—
no cash or C.O.D.'s please.

Name_____

Address_____

City_____State/Zip_____
Please allow four to six weeks for delivery. Offer good in U.S.A. only. Sorry, mail order not available to residents of Canada. Prices subject to change.   CAN987

Best friends, crushes, and lots of fun!

JUNIOR HIGH®
by Kate Kenyon

Get ready for lots of junior high madness at Cedar Groves Junior High! Laugh at best friends Nora and Jen's "cool" attempts to fit in. Cringe at the exceptionally gross tricks of Jason, the class nerd. Be awed by Mia who shows up on the first day of 8th grade in a punk outfit. And meet Denise, "Miss Sophistication," who shocks Nora and Jen by suggesting they invite BOYS to the Halloween party!

Get ready for the funny side of life in **Junior High!**

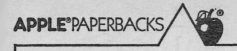

APPLE®PAPERBACKS

More books you'll love, filled with mystery, adventure, drama, and fun!

For Ages 11-13...

☐ 40054-1	**A, My Name Is Ami** Norma Fox Mazer	**$2.25**
☐ 40321-4	**Aliens in the Family** Margaret Mahy	**$2.50**
☐ 40055-X	**B, My Name Is Bunny** Norma Fox Mazer	**$2.50**
☐ 40241-2	**Baby-Snatcher** Susan Terris	**$2.50**
☐ 40849-6	**Fifteen at Last** Candice F. Ransom	**$2.50**
☐ 40501-2	**Fourteen and Holding** Candice F. Ransom	**$2.50**
☐ 40757-0	**Friends Are Like That** Patricia Hermes	**$2.50**
☐ 40129-7	**More Two-Minute Mysteries** Donald J. Sobol	**$2.25**
☐ 40352-4	**Our Man Weston** Gordon Korman	**$2.25**
☐ 33179-5	**The Rah Rah Girl** Caroline B. Cooney	**$2.50**
☐ 40192-0	**Thirteen** Candice F. Ransom	**$2.50**
☐ 41292-2	**Two-Minute Mysteries** Donald J. Sobol	**$2.50**
☐ 40589-6	**With You and Without You** Ann M. Martin	**$2.50**

Available wherever you buy books... or use the coupon below.